The Zone

Jada Tan Rufo

ISBN-10:1548407518
ISBN-13:9781548407513

To the Women of Nanjing

May you rest in peace.

To Norm,
Mahalo!

CONTENTS

Acknowledgments

Forward

Notes

I'D LIKE TO THANK MY WRITER'S
SUPPORT GROUP AND THE HAWAII
WRITER'S GUILD FOR THEIR
CONTINUED AND UNWAVERING
SUPPORT IN WRITING THIS VERY
CHALLENGING BOOK.

Forward

     November 2016. Like many of you I watched the election results with baited breath. And like half of the people in this country I was emotionally drained at the results.

     What happened?

     Prior to the election my personal Facebook page was filled with doomsday memes and posts. One post was about the Japanese interment camps. When Donald Trump made a reference to establishing a Muslim registry and detaining Muslims a picture of three young Japanese American boys standing behind a barbed wire fence showed up on my feed. When Trump labeled news organizations as "fake" to show his disagreement with reporters, a black-and-white photo of Hitler addressing the crowd with the phrase *luggen presse* (lying press) showed up. Are we seriously returning to our ugly past?

As time went on into Trump's presidency I knew I'd better get on the stick and complete *The Zone* as soon as possible. History does not need to repeat itself when it comes to discrimination and press freedoms. Atrocities tied to racist ideology certainly do not deserve an encore.

December 2017 marks the 80th anniversary of the Rape of Nanjing. On December 12th, 1937, the city fell to the Japanese Imperial Army. What followed was six weeks of hell on earth. The Japanese would search the Safety Zone for Chinese soldiers. They constantly harassed those who were trying to help Chinese refugees and they beheaded victims at will. They did this under the banner of "friendship" and ending western imperialism. They also believed that they were the superior race over the Chinese referring to them as "pigs" and "dogs".

But it is the women of Nanjing who suffered the most.

If travelers were to visit Nanjing today they will find that the street layout is basically unchanged. Many of the buildings on Nanjing Normal University, site of the former Ginling Women's College, are unchanged. The Quadrangle is also there. The campus certainly has grown but many of the buildings from that time period are still there. They will also find John Rabe's house which is now a museum and a center for peace. They may also find Gulou Hospital where Dr. Robert Wilson worked. It is still there as a working hospital.

What is new is the Nanjing Massacre Memorial which sits on the largest massacre site in the city. It is much like our Vietnam Memorial Wall in that that there are several slabs of granite with names of victims engraved. There is also a museum depicting events of those dark days from the air raids to the war crimes tribunal. This is also Rabe's final resting place.

One of the most striking features of the Memorial is the number of dead: 300,000. To me that represented 300,000 untold stories and scenarios that could have happened to any Nanjing family. This is a work of fiction. Yet it is a historical novel. This story is written from the prospective of two fictitious families based on survivors' accounts and photographs from Yale School of Divinity's Nanjing Project website and the diaries of John Rabe and

Minnie Vautrin. My purpose in writing in this manner is to get a glimpse of how everyday people experienced the war and to visualize their agony as they are forced to watch family members raped and killed right before their eyes.

Dying is easy. It's living that's hard.

Jada Tan Rufo

November,2017

Notes

      The western world learned about Nanjing, also known as Nanking, in 1842 at the end of the first Opium war with Britain through the signing of the *Treaty of Nanking*. The signing took place aboard the HMS Cornwallis which was anchored in the city. In China it is known as an "unequal treaty" because Britain was not required to do anything. China, however, was forced to cede portions of its territory. The most notable was the ceding of Hong Kong which China agreed to lease it rent free to Britain for one hundred years.

      This treaty also allowed other western countries to take advantage of the Qing government's ignorance of the west by negotiating unequal treaties of their own and it allowed foreigners in China to live as if there were in their home countries. This practice is known as extra territoriality. If a foreign national were to commit a crime against a Chinese that national would be tried under his home country's laws. However, if a Chinese national were to commit a crime against a westerner that Chinese would be tried under western law even though the crime was committed on Chinese soil.

Extra territoriality also allowed foreigners to conduct business anywhere they pleased with no restrictions. Religious organizations could proselyte anywhere they wanted and western businesses can set up shop where ever they pleased. If they ran into Chinese resistance they could rely on their governments to send in western troops, which is what happened in the Boxer Rebellion where members of the Righteous and Harmonious Fists, a.k.a the Boxers, staged a rebellion against Christian churches in Shandong Province. Religious organizations and western businesses came in droves. Chinese had no say in the negotiations. All they could do was comply with western demands to open up their borders. As a result in today's China missionary work is strictly prohibited and foreigners can no longer own a business unless a Chinese partner is involved.

Japan touted itself as China's savior. They made false promises claiming that they would help its neighbor to expel western interests and to share in the spoils. This idea led to the Greater East Asia Co-Prosperity Sphere concept and the phrase "Asia for Asians".

One ardent believer in this idea was General Iwane Matsui who fought in Manchuria in the Russo-Japanese War of 1904 and had assisted Chiang Kai Shek, known in China as Jiang Jieshi, in moving to Japan.

Meanwhile relations between China and Japan further deteriorated when Japan invaded Manchuria in 1931 and turned it into a puppet state called Manchukuo and placing the boy emperor Pu Yi as head of state. But they needed a reason to invade the rest of China. They got it when in July of 1937 a Japanese soldier had gone missing in a small town Wanping 10.2 miles southwest of Beijing near the Marco Polo Bridge. The Japanese commander demanded to search the town for the soldier but the Chinese refused. Although the missing soldier returned safely to his barracks both armies had already mobilized and the first shot was fired by the Chinese. This is regarded as China's entry into the Second World War. In China it is also know as the War of Resistance Against Japan.

Nanjing was the capital of Nationalist or Guomindang China. By then Matsui had come out of retirement and was placed in command of Japan's campaign on eastern and southern China. Chiang was kidnapped and taken to Xi'an to sign a peace treaty with his arch rival Mao Zedong the Communist leader of China. Although these two men were bitter enemies they thought it best to lay down their arms against each other and instead fight the Japanese.

This infuriated Matsui who saw Chiang's signing of the treaty as a betrayal of friendship. Matsui saw Nanjing as his for the taking and was eager to lead the campaign in eastern China all along the Yangtze River from Shanghai to Nanjing. In every town and village the Japanese conquered they subjected the Chinese to their three alls policy – kill all, burn all, and loot all. They killed men and boys, raped their women folk, stole their possessions, and burned what was left. They did this because their army was moving faster than their supply lines and they were always running out of food and other resources. Furthermore they needed an incentive for soldiers to stay in the army and told them that they could keep the spoils from the towns they invaded.

Meanwhile the Japanese air force ran an air raid campaign on the capital. Nanjing's population fell considerably from 1,000,000 people. Those who had the means to flee fled. Those who remained were poor and had no where else to go. From August to December of 1937 the city was subject to constant air raids thus preparing the way for the ground attack. Refugees from other towns along the Yangtze River basin would flee to Nanjing thinking they

8

would be safe. At the same time there were refugees fleeing the city which is why it is difficult to find any resource about the population of Nanjing in December of 1937. Figures range from as low as 150,000 to 500,000 during the massacre.

Days prior to the invasion Chiang moved his government to Chongqing in central China. Before leaving the city all administrative functions were turned over to John Rabe, a German businessman working for the Siemens Company. Rabe and twenty-two other westerners defied their governments' orders to leave China. To them, remaining in the city to help victims in their time of need was an opportunity to give service of the highest kind. It was a question of morality and doing the right thing. In order to save the remaining population of Nanjing they created an International Safety Zone under the hospices of the International Red Cross, much to the consternation of the Japanese authorities. Just before evacuating with the Guomindang Mayor Ma ordered all residents to take refugee in the Zone.

On December 12th, just hours before the fall of the city the *USS Panay*, a gunboat ship carrying foreign reporters and western embassy staff away from Nanjing, was bombed in a Japanese air raid several miles downriver heading to Shanghai. The attack killed three passengers and forced survivors to seek medical help in a rural village along the Yangtze River before being rescued by the British ship *Ladybird* and the *USS Oahu*.

Hours later Japanese guns could be heard pounding the south and the east of the city just outside Nanjing's ancient city walls. Chinese forces defending the city were overwhelmed and soundly defeated. Chinese soldiers ended up throwing away their uniforms and putting on civilian clothes to blend in with the locals.

On December 12th Zhonghua and Guanghua Gates were breached and Japanese soldiers entered the city. Minnie Vautrin, the American dean of Ginling Women's College beautifully sums up the mood of the city as she wrote in her diary the following entry for December 13th:

> The city is strangely silent – after all the bombing and shelling. Three dangers are past – that of looting soldiers, bombing from aeroplanes, and shelling from big guns, but the fourth is still before us --- our fate at the hands of the victorious army. People are very anxious tonight and to not know what to expect.

Later that night Vautrin continues her diary entry:

Tonight Nanking has no lights, no water, no telephone, no telegraph, no city paper, no radio. We are indeed separated from all of you by an impenetrable zone.

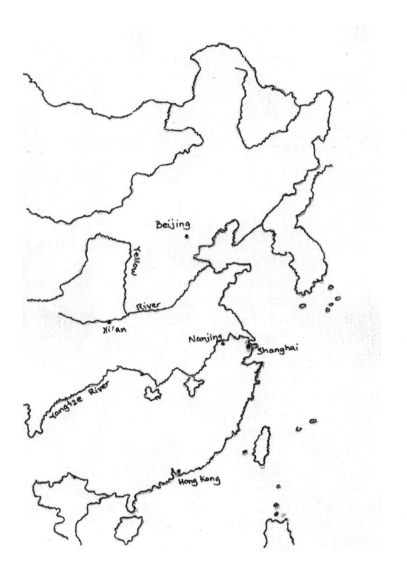

Map of China

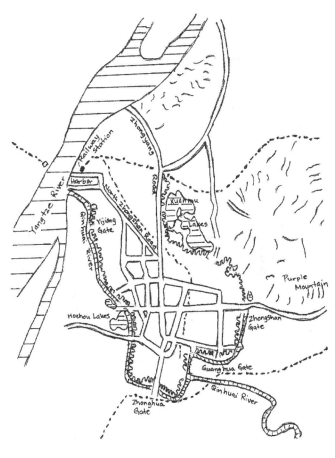

Nanjing

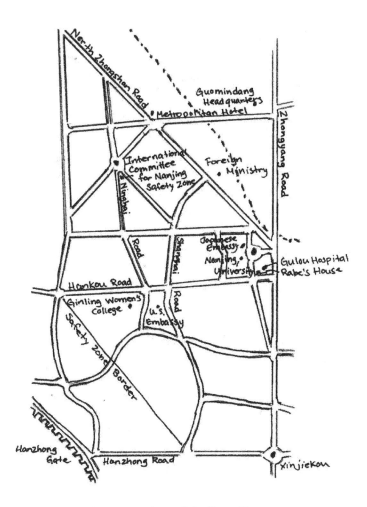

International Safety Zone

Map of Ginling Women's College

1. Quadrangle
2. Reception Hall & Gymnasium (Central Building)
3. Science Building
4. Chapel & Music Hall
5. 600 Dormitory
6. 400 Dormitory
7. Faculty House
8. 700 Dormitory
9. Arts Building
10. Library   &   Administration

Chapter One

Eeee yooo eeee yooo eeee yoooo!

Xue sits straight up from her steel frame bunk bed at the sound of the siren. The August sun shines brightly through their window and on to the concrete dormitory floor.

Rrrrrrrrrrrat-tat-tat-tat-tat!

She turns to her friend Ling lying on the bed below hers. "You hear that?" Xue whispers.

In a distance a loud BOOM goes off.

Ling turns, rubs her eyes and faces her friend. "Wha..?"

Rrrrrrrrrrrat-tat-tat-tat-tat-tat.

Xue quickly scrambles down her ladder and opens the window. Even the wooden table in front of the window cannot prevent Xue from checking out the action outside. She sticks her head out and looks up into the sky.

A single fighter plane strafes the Nanjing skyline. The plane is so low that Xue can see the pilot's face as he brushes above the rooftops of Ginling Women's College – their school. Xue can't quite make out if the airplane is Chinese or Japanese.

She didn't need to.

"They're…"

Xue pulls back inside to warn her roommates just as the pilot fires a series of bullets. One brushes Xue's hair and hits the wooden door. Another embeds itself in the table. Xue ducks and takes cover on the floor. The others cover themselves with blankets or pillows on their beds.

The door and table ignite.

By now all four girls in the room are awake and scrambling to put out the fires. Meng, the oldest girl in the room, grabs a pillow, races down her ladder and smothers the fire on the door with the pillow while Ling, Xue, and Yujie extinguish the fire on the table with water in their tin mugs and thermoses.

Eeeeee yooooo eeeeee yoooooo eeeeeee yoooooo!

Outside Yang Ayi pounds on their door and barks out orders. "Girls! Get up! Go to the Central Building basement! Now! We are under attack!"

Yujie is furious. Although she is the shortest girl, she makes her presence known with her shrill, high pitched voice. She turns and glares at Xue who is now cowering.

"You whore!"

Xue is taken aback by Yujie's anger. Although Xue is used to being called by such an ugly name she is puzzled.

How does she know me? We've only met two days ago.

Yang Ayi's booming voice from the hallway moves to the next door and repeats the order.

"Get up! Go to the Central Building! Now! Let's go! Let's go!"

"We're coming!" Meng yells through the door. "Look," she says to her roommates. "Fighting and name calling won't help! Let's go!"

Meng opens the door Girls are now pouring into the hallway. Two are seriously injured. One has been hit in the leg and is screaming her lungs out. Another has been hit in the shoulder and passes out at the sight of her own blood. Level headed Meng volunteers along with another girl from another room to take the student with a shoulder injury to the Central Building. Two other volunteers carry the screaming girl downstairs and on to the Central Building leaving the rest of the students with Yang Ayi.

"What's happening?" one girl asks as they all head to the stairs.

"Didn't Miss Vautrin say that there wouldn't…"

"Move it!" Yang Ayi yells.

The girls, including Ling, Xue, and Yujie run down the nearest flight of stairs to the first floor where more girls are waiting to be called.

Yang Ayi takes the roll call.

"Han Xue?"

"Here."

"Tan Ling?"

"Here."

"Sun Yujie?"

"Here."

All ambulatory students in Dormitory 400 are accounted for.

BOOM!

Exploding bombs could be heard in a distance followed by more planes flying in single fire formation and rapid gun fire.

Rat-tat-tat-tat.

"Walk in a single file, girls," Yang Ayi orders them. "Stick with your friend."

All the girls follow Yang Ayi, a stocky older woman and a dorm worker in her mid-fifties. They follow her like chicks following their mother to safety as they all take cover in the Central Building on Ginling Women's College.

The college itself is in disarray especially behind Dormitory 600 where workers are constructing a trench behind the building and in the Science Building where faculty and staff are moving things to the basement. There are workers with hoes, shovels, and picks standing in the Quadrangle, the open lawn area directly in front of the Central Building. They are looking at the sky. Workers in the Science Building are moving crates full of beakers and tungsten burners. Some of the workers drop their crates full of microscopes and run to the action as if they were watching a sporting event.

There are other workers pushing wheel barrels filled with sand bags who have stopped to watch the air raid. No one has ever seen anything like it.

"What the hell are you doing?" someone screams. "Run!"

As they walk some girls peer out from beneath the

covered walkway leading to the Central Building to see what is happening on such a clear hot August summer.

A single plane strafes the Nanjing skyline spraying bullets.

Rrrrrrrat-tat-tat-tat-tat.

Who or what this plane is firing at is anyone's guess. But some of the workers fall to the ground.

"Are they dead?" one girl asks.

"Stay in line!" Yang Ayi orders the students.

Students from Dormitories 600 and 700 are also taking shelter in the basement of the Central Building beneath the ground floor. Some are clearly confused. Others are screaming and covering their ears at the sound of the firing bullets and detonating bombs. Still others want to watch the air raid.

"I thought there weren't going to be any air raids."

"What's happening?"

All sixty girls chatter among themselves as they take their assigned places in the basement.

"Whose planes are they?" one girl asks.

"Tao yan guizi!"

Damn those devils!

Chapter Two

Eeeeee yoooo eeee yoooo!

     The siren wails all day long. It's a full assault on people's ears and nerves as it continuously emits its annoying warning thus disrupting their day as they go about their business.

     Or try to.

     Enemy planes strafe the sky. Sometimes a single plane leads the assault. Sometimes a cluster of them fire indiscriminately. Nonetheless the assault is never ending.

     BOOM!

The ground ungulates as bombs detonate inside the ancient city walls. These walls that have protected the people from a ground invasion are no match for aerial warfare. Planes drop their explosive cargo on military targets inside the city including the airfield as well as Xinjiekou, Nanjing's commercial center. Shops and businesses all along Zhongshan and Hanzhong Roads explode. Buildings tumble. Fires burn.

On the street chaos reigns as people run for cover. Air raids have now become a part of life in Nanjing. If the siren goes off they have been trained to seek shelter in an underground bunker even if it turns out to be a false alarm. Public transportation operators have been ordered to drive their passengers to the nearest bomb shelter and abandon their vehicles if the roads are clear. If not, they are to shelter in place until the all-clear signal is given.

The bombing is relentless. Dog fights ensue. Chinese fighter pilots scramble to defend their skies. Their aerial display is breathtaking but dangerous.

But no one is watching. Beautifully dressed women run for cover. Some drop their merchandise on the street at the sound of the siren. Children struggle to keep up with their mothers. A toddler falls face forward on the pavement screaming. A rickshaw driver stumbles and falls from shrapnel. His carriage topples on its side leaving his two passengers to fend for themselves.

All three are dead.

Exhausted emergency crews are out in full force guiding people to shelters. Fire brigades are called upon to extinguish fires at Central Hospital and the radio station. They are fighting a losing battle. Buildings crumble and they pull out more charred bodies than survivors.

Central Hospital is under siege even under the banner of a Red Cross flag sprawled on its roof. Staff scramble to rush patients to the basement away from windows.

The earth constantly vibrates from bombs falling and buildings toppling. A man, a beggar, sits on the sidewalk behind a sign that is written in chalk on the sidewalk.

My name is Wang. I have no home. I have no family. I have nothing. Please help.

The man sits there with a tin mug. He bangs it on the pavement to get attention. But no one is listening. People run all over his sign. The man is oblivious to the bombing until a young man stops to assist him.

"Let me help you, uncle," says the young man.

The beggar suddenly awakens from his stupor by this young man who takes his arm and helps the beggar to his feet.

A plane drops a bomb hitting its target. Shrapnel and debris from the attack fly everywhere. The two men fall over.

Dead.

Their blood trickles through the man's name, a sign of his misfortune.

It is a sign of the misfortune yet to come.

The faint all-clear signal has just been given. After seven hours of relentless bombing the Japanese have retreated to their bases.

But it is still dangerous to leave any shelter. Telephone lines are down and roads are blocked. But these are the least of people's worries.

East of the Metropolitan Hotel is a bombed rail line. The Japanese have bombed every track and station along the city rail line and the line to Beijing. Buildings around the target areas have endured heavy damage due to fire or to seismic activity from bombs hitting their targets and detonating. The smell of burning ammunition, metal, wood, and concrete permeates the air. Buildings are reduced to smoldering rubble. There is no water since the pumping station was also targeted. All fire crews can do is let Nanjing burn itself out and keep residents in air raid shelters.

Local fire and safety officials in Gulou open the bunkers and air raid shelters later in the afternoon. After being cooped up for seven hours people are anxious to stretch their legs and see the light. Little do they know that the world above them has drastically changed.

Ironically the Metropolitan Hotel sustained little damage. But that offers very little comfort and no one bothers to take notice. Employees working the front desk do what they can under flickering lights. Guests are running down the staircase lugging their belongings in suitcases and bags. Elevators are out. Visitors emphatically slam their keys on the counter as clerks hurry to complete transactions while it is still daylight.

As Meizhen and Xue venture out of their shelter they see Master Han, his wife Madame Han, and their son Rong outside the hotel entrance loading their treasures in a donkey drawn cart and paying the farmer for the use of his animal and wagon. After the farmer leaves with his donkey and cart the family's chauffeur shows up in a Rolls-Royce.

"Master!" Meizhen pleads as she and Xue run and kowtow to him and his family. "Please! I beg you to take us with you! We have no where else to go! We will die here!"

Master Han is clearly embarrassed to be seen in the same space with his employee and former lover. At first he tries to ignore her. But when the two women kowtow a second time right at his feet begging and weeping he is forced to do something on the spot.

"Rong?" He signals for his son. "Bring the briefcase."

Rong brings the leather briefcase to his father. He holds it up to his father while Master Han fiddles with the combination lock to open in. The lock clicks and Master Han opens the case to reveal stacks of yuan bills all tightly bound in paper and neatly aligned in rows. He takes two wads of cash and hands them over to Meizhen.

"Here," he says. "Your last month's salary. For you and the girl."

Meizhen slowly looks up through her tear-stained face.

Why is he giving me this money? He's already paid me for this month.

"Please take us!" she screams.

"I-I-I can't," Master Han stammers clearly embarrassed that this is happening out in the open.

"Then please take Xue," Meizhen begs. "She is your flesh and blood. She even carries your family's name. Han Xue."

Master Han looks down at Xue who has not moved an inch.

"She is not my daughter."

He tosses Meizhen the cash on the ground and tries to turn away. By this time the chauffeur has opened the back door of the car but the family has yet to get in. Meizhen quickly rises to her feet, picks up a wad of bills and throws them at Master Han hitting him square in the back.

"Cao zhi!" she screams.

Master Han looks over his shoulder. "What did you say?"

"*Cao zhi!*" Meizhen repeats. "Useless! Good for wiping your ass!"

Madame Han then steps in. She is now nose-to-nose with Meizhen and slaps her hard on her face.

"You ungrateful bitch!" Madame yells. "After all that we've done for you! We took you in from the hinterlands. We trained you. We fed you and clothed you. This is what we get? You can at least take your money and exchange it at the exchange center.

Meizhen slowly regains her composure and looks at Xue who remains on her knees with her face down.

"Very well. Xue? Pick up the *cao zhi*. Let's go."

Xue crawls on the ground picking up the two wads of cash before rising to her feet. Master Han, Madame, and their son get in the back of their car. Meizhen stops the chauffeur from closing the door.

"If we are killed by the devils then you will have blood on your hands. Try living with that for the rest of your lives."

She slams the door. The chauffeur gets in and starts the car before driving off leaving Meizhen and her daughter to fend for themselves outside the hotel lobby. They sat on the stairs wondering what to do next as the hotel quickly empties of guests leaving only a small staff on duty. To ease her nerves Meizhen opens her handbag and takes out a cigarette and a lighter. She lights up her cigarette as a weary Xue leans on her mother's shoulder.

"Ling has a grandma and a grandpa," says Xue. "Where are my grandparents? How come I've never met them?"

Meizhen slowly inhales and exhales. "I have no memory of my parents," she replies. "Darling, don't let anyone treat you like property. You are a human being. Just because you are a girl doesn't mean people can treat you like an animal. Fight for what you want. Fight for what you believe in because I believe in you."

"I believe in you too, Mama. I believe in you."

Chapter Three

The Tan family dinner is always a sumptuous affair. After closing the restaurant at 8 p.m. the family would clean off a round table with a wet cloth and the children would set the chairs around the table. Ling and Jun would prepare the table with plates, bowls, tea cups, and chopsticks. Mama, Nai Nai, and Aunty would bring out the dishes from the restaurant kitchen. Ye Ye, Baba, and sometimes Uncle would be in the kitchen cooking. The smell of crushed garlic permeated the air. The sound of the roaring fire and Ye Ye frying eggs, vegetables, rice, or meat in hot oil could be heard from across the street.

But how long would this feast last? That is the question that looms on every adult's mind as the family sits down for dinner. The question is especially pressing for Uncle.

"It's getting more difficult to get supplies these days. The markets are selling less items but at such outrageous prices. Yesterday, one *jin* of pork was 100 yuan. Today it's 350. Who knows how much it will cost tomorrow?"

"The devils are closing in on Zhenjiang Town," Ye Ye adds. "I've been listening to the reports."

"I got tonight's meal from my best supplier," Uncle Tan continues. "This was all he had. No pork. Just chicken and vegetables. Not even fruit for the children.

"He said, 'I would rather give this to you than sell it.'" Uncle stuffs his mouth with rice before going on. "The devils raided his neighbor's fields and took his friend's family. He hid his wife and children in their bunker. He ordered his family to poison their livestock. When he gets back he will leave the farm with his family and burn their house and crops. Nothing will be left for the devils."

"Yes," Baba solemnly replies. "We may have to close the restaurant. I may have to find another job."

The noodle restaurant is Baba's blood, sweat, and tears. The thought of closing it sickens him. But the thought of the Japanese looting it should it remain open makes Baba even sicker. To see his career end at the hands of those devils was far worse that closing the establishment and finding a job.

But at his age and with the economy on the brink of disaster due to the fighting in the country what could he do? No one has money. No one has jobs unless they work for the Japanese.

Jun, on the other hand, is itching to say something. However, he is afraid as to what Baba might say. Jun waits for the right time. Here it is.

"I have an idea."

"Hmm," Baba mumbles as he fiddles with his food using his chopsticks. He doesn't even flinch. "What is it?"

"My head teacher met with us boys in my class yesterday morning." Jun waits for Baba's reaction. Baba keeps stuffing his mouth with rice.

"And?"

"He says the Guomindang need men."

Nai Nai senses the tension. She cannot stand such conflict especially when it has to do with death. Already the city has endured weeks of constant air raids and an exodus of refugees and foreigners fleeing.

"Must we talk about this?" Nai Nai asks.

Ye Ye is indignant. Although he did not want to talk about it with the family, especially in front of Xiao Jian and Xiao Wei, this was something that could not be avoided. "Quiet, old woman! Our grandson wants to talk about this. It's important to him."

Ye Ye didn't want the conflict anymore than his wife. But this is the family's reality. This is the world he and Nai Nai are leaving their grandchildren. Jun joining the fight had to be discussed.

Jun is grateful for Ye Ye's interference. Jun smiles at Ye Ye as Jun sticks a piece of chicken in his mouth with a pair of chopsticks. It may be his last bit of home cooking before returning to school.

It may be his last home meal. Period.

"I'll get a stipend to send home."

"No." Baba stops Jun from going any further. "Your place is here with your family. Protect your sister."

"But Baba. She has Ye Ye, Uncle Tan, and you!"

Baba firmly puts down his chopsticks and bowl on the table and stared at his son. "No!"

As the first born in his family Baba is expected to look after his parents. He is expected to take over the noodle restaurant after Ye Ye and Nai Nai leave this world. He also expects his own eldest son Jun to do the same.

However, it is clear to everyone that Jun had other ideas. He immediately stands up and abruptly leaves the table bolting out the door and taking his jacket with him.

Everyone is stunned. The tense atmosphere gives way to dead silence. The clatter of bowls and chopsticks ceases. No one speaks.

Xiao Wei's cooing finally breaks the silence and the family resumes eating. No one speaks for the rest of the meal.

At the end of the meal Ye Ye and Nai Nai take their grandchildren to their private apartment above the restaurant while Baba, Mama, and Uncle remain to clean up and close. The atmosphere is tense.

"You will have to let Jun go sometime," says Mama. "You must talk to him before he returns to school tomorrow."

"Once he returns to school, that's it," Uncle adds. "You will never see him again."

Baba is furious. "Are you both telling me how to run my household?"

"You are a fine father," Mama said trying to appease her husband. "But Jun wants to fight the Japanese with his friends. They've all enlisted."

Baba is shocked to hear this coming from his own wife. "You are okay with this?" he asked.

"If it means that I'd have to sacrifice my own flesh and blood to get these devils out of Nanjing, then yes. I am okay with that."

"Well I am not!" You forget that is *my* son. Not just yours."

Mama sees she is getting nowhere with her husband. She doesn't want Jun to leave. She doesn't like unresolved issues to left without closure. She hates having conflict in her family. But she is getting tired of playing the peace maker role. She leaves that up to her brother-in-law.

"Ai ya!" Mama just throws down her rag in the sink and left.

It was up to Uncle Tan to make amends now.

"Brother, do you remember 1919?"

May 1919. Baba is a university student who was due to graduate in two months. He is on his way to the university dining hall when his brother comes running up to him with a university bulletin in his hand.

"Brother!" Uncle Tan pants. "Did you see this?"

Baba glances at the bulletin in his brother's hand.

Shandong ceded to Japan!

"Are you going to the demonstration?" Uncle Tan asks.

"Of course," Baba replies. "I'm just as angry as you. But I can't protest on an empty stomach."

After lunch the brothers take a bus to North Zhongshan Road where throngs of their fellow students have gathered to stage their protest. The very idea that the western powers had given Shandong Province, the province north of theirs, to Japan instead of returning it to China angered many students. Many had hoped that at the end of the Great War Shandong would be returned to the motherland.

Baba and Uncle Tan picked up signs made out of pieces of wood. One says "Shandong is OURS!" The other says "Down with Japan!"

Their fellow students also carry banners with much

*of the same message. Many of them shout in unison, "Down
with the western imperialism," or "Down with Japan". Their
destination is the Ministry of Foreign Affairs on North
Zhongshan Road.*

"This is Jun's fight, Brother," said Uncle. "Not ours.
Eventually you'll have to let him go."

Chapter Four

Public notice:

All Nanjing residents currently residing outside a designated safe zone must immediately evacuate their homes and seek refuge in the nearest safe zone.

Ma Chao Chun

Mayor of Nanjing

December 1st, 1937

Meizhen steps on the mayor's public notice leaving a dirty shoe print on the paper. She clutches Xue's hand as they navigate their way through downtown Nanjing. Both women are harried, dazed, exhausted, and confused along with other bewildered residents standing among the ruins of what was once a thriving city. Rumors abound with news of a safe zone in Nanjing. But no one seems to know if it is even allowed to exist. The westerners that have chosen to defy their home governments' orders to leave Nanjing have persistently petitioned the Japanese ambassador, Mr. Tanaka, to allow the International Safety Zone to exist. In order to appease the International Committee, led by John Rabe, Ambassador Tanaka replies by saying "things will get better". But the ambassador is unable to give Rabe a satisfactory answer since the Japanese army has all the power.

Hanzhong Road is teeming with people. Old men sit on the street wearing rags for clothes. They huddle next to a small fire as they beg for money, food, or clothes. But the fire is not enough to fight off the winter cold.

Shops have burned down and whatever goods they sold have already been looted by poor Chinese soldiers who don't even have the proper equipment to put up a fight. Many of the civilians don't even have shoes and must make do with old shoes, cloth torn from old clothing, or even straw.

Able bodied men and women carry their injured loved ones by bike, hastily made stretchers, or wooden carts. Some even transport injured children in straw baskets strapped to a bamboo pole carried by two men. Those who have no mode of transport carry their loved ones on their backs or in their arms. Some even enlist the help of strangers to help carry the infirmed. One grabs the arms while the other carries the legs. They use whatever they have to transport their injured family members to safety since the public transport system is now non-existent.

The atmosphere is pierced by the sounds of moaning, complaining, and cries for help as the injured are carried. Many are hurt from flying bits of concrete or brick as a result of the air raids. Some have burn injuries that have been allowed to fester for days. Civilians who have very little access to emergency services make do with what they have; homemade alcohol or traditional Chinese medicines. They have no way to get to a neighborhood clinic or to Gulou Hospital.

The young and the elderly are especially vulnerable. Old women worn with age and worry about their families struggle mightily as they hobble along the streets, some with younger family members in tow. But many others have no one to help them and depend on friends or strangers. Many weep as they leave their destroyed homes in search for the Safety Zone.

If it exists.

"Ma! Stop!" Xue screams. "I'm tired!"

Babies are also crying. Some scream for food. Others cry from their injuries. Still many others cry out of fear and resist leaving their burned out homes. This is all they know. Yet, that place that was once their safe haven is now gone.

Forever.

The two pass by young mothers trying in vain to ease their children's pain with whatever they have. They breast feed their children. They try to silence them with what little food they have. They try singing or playing games to get their young minds off the destruction. Parents struggle to keep their own emotions in check as they try to keep their children safe from harm.

But with all of Nanjing on the move the inevitable happens. Families separate because straggling family members can't keep up. Wives are separated from husbands. Children lose their parents. Toddlers sit on the road screaming while harried parents search for missing family members in vain.

"Keep moving!" Meizhen orders her resistant daughter. She holds Xue's hand with a vice-like grip.

A confused old woman approaches them. "Where is the Safety Zone?" she asks.

"I don't know," replies Meizhen who is just as confused and lost among the chaos and confusion.

A middle aged woman overhears the conversation. "I heard that the universities are in the Safety Zone," she chimes in.

"Are you sure?" Meizhen asks.

"Makes sense," the woman replies. "They are the only buildings left standing."

Although the Japanese military does not officially recognize the Safety Zone's existence they have refrained from bombing any building inside the Zone which includes American run institutions such as Nanjing University and Ginling Women's College where Xue is a student, the American, and Japanese Embassies, Gulou Hospital, and Rabe's home. Her best bet would be to head to the Women's College but to get there has proven difficult.

Ever since the Metropolitan Hotel, Meizhen employer and former place of residence, closed for business, the two women have been forced to move from place to place and around the city staying in friends' homes or in underground bunkers around the city. Her friend's home along the Qinhuai River in Mochou District on the south side of the city was razed to the ground by fire from the latest bombing raid forcing Meizhen to take refuge in an overcrowded underground bunker for a few days.

Now this edict from the mayor is forcing them to seek safety in a mysterious safe zone along with millions of other confused Nanjing-ren who aimlessly wander about with the same questions on their minds.

Thankfully they are on the east side of the river and are just inside city limits. Some of the other refugees have had to find inventive ways to cross the river. Many have reported seeing corpses on both sides of the river.

"I saw charred bodies floating in the river," claims one woman.

"I saw bodies of children floating in blood," said a man.

The two women escaped Meizhen's friend's home during last month's air raid thanks to the civil defense sirens going off. By now all of Nanjing, have gotten used to the sirens and the constant air raids. Her friend's home, however, was not so lucky. A bomb was dropped in the neighborhood causing several buildings, including her friend's home to shake and fall. The ensuing fire finished off the destruction. Thankfully casualties were minor thanks to the sirens. But Meizhen is heartbroken to see old women rummaging through the rubble of what was once their home. There is nothing to salvage but their dignity. All that is left are charred ruins, rats and stray dogs to pick up the pieces.

The two have a way to go to get Ginling Women's College. Although she is within the ancient city wall of Hanzhong Gate, the wall is not a part of the Safety Zone. Destruction and debris is everywhere and smoke rises from smoldering fires. Roads are blocked by debris including burned out vehicles.

Meizhen is weary. Carrying a leather suitcase with all of her possessions and dragging Xue into a war zone bogs her down as both women are forced to navigate the city on foot. Although she is wearing a *qipao* and a fur coat and her hair done as if she were to entertain hotel guests she is undone with sweat and soot. Her feet are cramped from walking or running. Her mascara is running down her once powdered cheeks as she desperately tries to reach the college. She half carries half drags her suitcase as she drags herself along Hanzhong Road.

Xue is also dragging a tattered leather suitcase. Her feet ache from continuous walking and although it is winter her sweat causes her body to stick to her clothes.

They are not alone in their search for the Safety Zone.

"Excuse me," she asks another woman. "Is the Women's College in the Safety Zone?"

"I don't know!" The woman dismisses her. "Mayor Ma issues an edict but he doesn't tell us where it is! Then he and Jiang Jieshi leave! Cowards!"

Hours before Mayor Ma and the Guomindang leave with their leader for Chongqing in central China, the mayor hands over all administrative duties to the International Safety Zone Committee. This includes all of the city's resources. The public utilities, police and fire, sanitation, and transportation sectors are now under the control of the Safety Zone Committee and its acting mayor, John Rabe.

Meizhen and Xue continue on slowly walking east on Hanzhong Road heading towards what was once the shopping district of Xinjiekou. On better days Meizhen would be riding the bus to Ginling Women's College to visit Xue. But now it is littered with downed telephone lines and Mayor Ma's leaflets. Buildings are deserted. But there are also a few that are left standing.

Are we getting closer?

By now Meizhen's mind is spinning as she is looking for a sign – any sign – of a standing building to just rest. She has been searching for the Safety Zone since dawn after a day of packing. Yesterday, the mayor issued his edict through leaflets that were dropped into the city and its surrounding areas, including Mochou District where Meizhen an Xue were staying before evacuating.

An army truck armed with a megaphone and a truck bed full of policemen plows through the streets. They occasionally stop to deploy officers to secure the streets or they are stopped by crowds closing in on them.

"Please go to a Red Cross Center," screams an officer over the megaphone.

The crowd of mainly women crowd in.

"Tell us where!" one woman yells.

"Look for any building with the Red Cross flag on it. You'll find shelter there. They can tell you where the Safety Zone is. We just saw flags posted at Nanjing University and at Ginling Women's College. Go there."

"We are tired!" another woman complained. "Can you take us?"

"I'm sorry. But we can't take all of you. Not enough room."

The truck moves on slowly through the street.

"Come on, ladies," said Meizhen. "They can't help us. They are only here to keep the streets safe, not to escort us to safety. I'm going to the Women's College. Follow me."

But the women hesitate. They give Meizhen that all too familiar stare. Old prejudices die hard, even in war.

"Seriously, ladies?" Meizhen asks them. "Are you really going to question me now?" I know where it is. I don't suppose you know how to get there," she says with a twinge of sarcasm in her voice.

Slowly and reluctantly the women accept Meizhen's offer and follow her and Xue to the college.

"I promise," says Meizhen. "Once we get there you will never see me again."

Haunting last words.

Chapter Five

John Rabe sits at his desk with his steel helmet on. A lantern is the only thing he has that allows him to work at night. The walls and windows of his three story home rattle and dust from the ceiling falls on his desk as the Japanese are now pounding Zhonghua Gate in the south and Guanghua Gate in the east. Both gates lead to the city center.

Rabe sits at his desk with a typewriter. He types in German:

Uninterrupted artillery fire from Purple Mountain. Thunder and lightening around the hill and suddenly the whole hill is in flames. They have set fire to some houses and a powder magazine. An old adage says:

When Purple Mountain burns, Nanjing is lost.(sic)

He continues on about how the Chinese troops at both gets come under heavy artillery fire before ending the paragraph with this observation:

But there can be no longer any doubt that the Japanese are at the gates and that the final push is about to start.

Outside on the street below groups of women crowd around Rabe's two gates rattling the steel bars creating a raucous noise. Their screaming and wailing is so intense that Rabe stops typing.

"Labei xiansheng! Qiu qiu ni ah. Kaimen!"

Mr. Rabe! Please! Open your gates!

Several women and children rattle the bars on Rabe's gates. Others kowtow on the sidewalks and on the street in front of his home. Rabe can no longer stand their crying and runs downstairs to open his home to the refugees. With the assistance of two Chinese colonels Long and Zhou who have also taken shelter in Rabe's compound, they allocate people to various places.

"Miss, take your son to dugout one," says Colonel Long to a haggard woman and her child.

"You're in dugout two," says Colonel Zhou to another weary woman.

Women and children overwhelm both dugouts in Rabe's garden. They bring with them their own bedding and a few precious belongings.

"Where shall we put them?" asks Colonel Long in English.

Rabe furiously paces around his garden trying to think on his feet. "Put them in the servant's quarters," he orders both colonels. "Once that is full then we can put them in the house."

The servant's quarters and the house quickly fill up as women and children occupy every square inch of every building. Only Rabe's office is devoid of people.

Yet they keep coming.

"Sir, where else can we put these women?" asks Colonel Zhou. "Your dugouts are full. Your servant's quarters are full. Your home is nearing capacity."

Rabe scratches his head. "Put them in my office."

So much for privacy and rest Rabe thought.

Still they keep coming. Rabe and the two colonels are forced to allow women and children to sleep out in the open in the winter weather. Some have taken refuge under the German flag believing it to be bomb proof. Still others even sleep on the cobblestone walkways that lead to the house and the servant's quarters. Every inch of Rabe's property is occupied by a woman or a child in need of a safe place. Rabe finds himself running from one end of the compound to the other ordering refugees to be quiet and comforting those who need comforting in a mixture of English, German, and broken Chinese.

Rabe resumes work on his diary. Suddenly a loud BOOM goes off at Zhonghua Gate in the south. There is a knock on the door downstairs. Rabe's fellow German Christian Kroger somehow manages to pick his way to the door amidst all the refugees. It is approaching midnight.

"Good Lord, Krischan," Rabe greets his friend using Kroger's nick name. "What are you doing here?"

"Just checking to see how you're doing," Kroger replies. "I just saw Zhongyang Road. What a mess! The street is littered with uniforms, military equipment, and all kinds of weapons left by Chinese troops. Seems like they are retreating."

Kroger leans on Rabe's desk. He fidgets with his jacket searching for something in his pocket. "Oh! Among other things someone has just given me a usable bus for 20 Mex[1] dollars." He takes out a huge wad of cash and runs his fingers through it. "Do you think we ought to take it?"

"Lord, Krischan! You can't be serious!"

---

[1]Some of China's currency was minted in Mexico.

"Well, I've told the man to stop by the office tomorrow sometime."

Rabe is flabbergasted at the outrageous but generous offer.

"I was able to exchange some Reich marks for Mex dollars at the Exchange before they closed," Kroger continues as he puts his money back inside his jacket.

"What do you plan to do with this bus?"

Kroger folds his arms and looks around the crowded office. "Well, it could be a refugee house or a transport vehicle for food supplies." He spots Rabe's insulin needles and bottles on Rabe's desk. "How about a mobile hospital unit? Our American friend Dr. Wilson would love that."

Rabe cringes at that name. When the International Safety Zone Committee nominated Rabe as its chairman, Dr. Robert Wilson was the only one who objected the nomination.

"Great!" exclaimed Wilson sarcastically. "Now we have a Nazi as *der Fuher* of our Safety Zone!"

"I wouldn't worry about the doctor," said Kroger. "That's Robert being Robert. He hates the fact that you are a member of the Nazi Party. But he respects you as a human being. If I were you I'd worry about the Japanese than Dr. Wilson."

"I already am," replies Rabe. "I keep getting these telegrams from the German Embassy regarding the Japanese recognition of our Zone. Tepid at best."

"Let's just hope they would at least stay away," said Kroger. "Well, I should be on my way."

"No! Please stay!" Rabe insists. "It isn't safe."

Kroger laughs as he looks around Rabe's office packed to the brim with sleeping refugees. "You have no room! Besides I have my armband," he chuckles as he slaps his Nazi swastika on his right shoulder. "What can the Japanese do to us? We're Germans!" Kroger laughs before leaving his friend.

Under normal circumstances Rabe, who loves jokes, would have laughed at wise cracks like that. But after two days of constant cannon and machine gun fire and after struggling through the day-to-day logistics of running the Safety Zone, Rabe has no time for a decent night of sleep. As chairman of the International Safety Zone Committee his duties include negotiating with the Japanese to at least allow the Zone to exist. But so far his efforts have proven futile.

Taking naps is impossible since the bombardment is continuous. He has no time change his clothes. Even packing for an emergency is done in haste as Rabe stuffs his medical bag with his insulin and bandages. He writes:

Every joint in my body hurts. I have not been out of these clothes for forty-eight hours. My guests are settling in for the night as well. Around thirty people are asleep in my office, three in the coal bin, eight women and children in the servant's quarters, and the rest, over a hundred people, are in the dugouts or out in the open, in the garden, on the cobblestones, everywhere!

Meanwhile at Ginling Women's College Minnie Vautrin is also awake due to the constant shelling of the city gates. She writes in her diary:

Few people will sleep in the city tonight. From the South Hill Residence we could see the South City still burning and also Xiaguan. Think I shall sleep with my clothes on tonight so I can get up if I am needed. Wish the night were over.

Chapter Six

Nanjing. Hours after its fall. Smoke emerges from the south and fires are still smoldering on Purple Mountain in the east.

When Purple Mountain burns, Nanjing is lost.

The Japanese have taken control of several city gates. They have yet to take the city center. It's just a matter of hours before anarchy rules.

The soldiers move in groups of ten to twenty men into Xinjiekou, the shopping district of Nanjing. There are reports of soldiers smashing and grabbing items from stores before setting buildings on fire. Soldiers are seen loading their loot in crates. They also commandeer anything with wheels and load their stolen goods.

The streets are nearly deserted. Only a few, brave souls are out and about searching for provisions to last through the day. Members of the International Safety Zone Committee are also taking a tour of the entire city. There are reports of wide spread looting outside the Safety Zone including the raiding of a home belonging to an American missionary family on Taiping Road.

One cannot avoid the corpses littering the streets. There are several decomposing bodies every two hundred meters or so. Some of them have bullet holes in the back, indicating they were shot while fleeing.

Skinny, stray dogs roam the city gorging on human flesh. There is no shortage of food as dogs lie on the street ripping human remains clean off the bone. They travel in packs as they now resort to their wild instincts of their canine ancestors.

They are harmless compared to the human wolves that carry *katanas* and bayonets and roam the streets of Nanjing unchecked and untamed.

Baba and Uncle Tan try to cover their noses and mouths with their clothes as they walk along Shanghai Road, pushing their empty tricycle cart. There is no point in riding their tricycle since the street is also covered with discarded military gear left by fleeing Chinese soldiers as well as corpses. The danger of running over a grenade or hitting a bomb is real. This is their reality.

San guang zheng ce.

"They are enforcing their three alls policy," whispers Baba.

Sha guang, xiao guang, qiang guang.

Kill all, burn all, loot all.

The brothers keep their eyes and ears open peeled for friends in need of assistance as well as enemy soldiers. Although they live in the Safety Zone and although the Japanese have not attacked the Zone due to the dogged persistence of the International Safety Zone Committee, soldiers still enter and commit unspeakable atrocities.

It is anything but safe. But it is better than living outside the Zone where Japanese soldiers can do what they like because there is no international presence there.

The brothers slowly walk the street pushing their tricycle to avoid any accidents. They encounter body after body. Some of them have been stripped of their belongings. Those that are clothed were once owners of gray or black, puffy down jackets and winter pants that are now drenched with dried, caked blood. The stench is unbearable. Many have missing body parts. Some have had their eyes gouged out, tongues cut, and ears chopped. Others were sliced open exposing intestines, stomachs, hearts, and lungs.

Some have been beheaded.

But the corpses of women are the most disturbing to the brothers. Like the men some are partially clothed. Some lie naked on the cold, hard pavement. Many have been mutilated much like the men; missing body parts and missing heads. They lie on their backs, breasts exposed, and legs apart. However the shocking difference is that some women have *katanas* shoved up their vaginas. Others have been spared such humiliation and torture but show evidence of a bayonet blade thrust into their cervixes. Still others were clearly bayoneted in their abdomens.

Baba's stomach churns and Uncle winces. If the Japanese could do this without a conscience, then there is no hope for Nanjing's women like Ling and Aunty Shen and her unborn child.

In a distance is a group of Japanese soldiers laughing and smoking. In their midst is a naked woman in her twenties. The soldiers had just raped her and dragged her out on to the street. While it is winter, there is no snow but it is cold as she is folding her arms to keep warm and is trying desperately to cover her breasts at the same time.

"What are they doing" Baba asks, straining to see what one of the soldiers is holding in his hands.

The soldier holds a camera to his face. His friends laugh while he is taking a picture of the poor woman.

"*Tian na*! My god!" whispers Uncle.

"Don't look," says Baba.

The brothers slowly and methodically walk up the street, pushing their cart north on Shanghai Road. They try not to draw any attention to themselves as they search for victims in need of assistance as well as scraps of food for their family.

They encounter more corpses than survivors.

"That's Old Mu!" Uncle Tan exclaims as they pass the body of Old Mu.

Old Mu. Ye Ye's drinking and smoking buddy. They would play cards on Saturdays in their apartment above the restaurant.

Old Mu. *Si le.* Dead.

"Don't tell Father about this," whispers Baba.

Just a few meters away from Old Mu's body lies a corpse of a teenage boy dressed in school uniform; the same uniform as Jun. The boy is lying face down with bullet holes in his back. His once crisp uniform is covered in blood.

"Oh, my god!" Baba runs towards the lifeless boy. He struggles to turn the body over.

Just as he and Uncle turn the corpse over, he hears a click and stares down the barrel of a pistol. The man holding the weapon is a young Japanese soldier with a scowl on his face. Behind him are several of his comrades with their bayonets fixed on their weapons' some of them are already dripping with the blood of innocent victims.

The soldier holding the gun speaks in broken Chinese.

"You! Soldier!"

"*Bu shi*!" Uncle argues. "We're not…"

Before he could finish his sentence the scowling soldier points the gun at Uncle's face.

"Tie them up and load them in the truck," the soldier ordered his comrades. "These two can be diggers. Take their cart."

The others do as ordered. They tie Baba and Uncle's hands behind their backs and force the two Chinese men into the back of a truck, prodding the two captives with their bayonets at their backs. Baba and Uncle are the first two captives but the truck bed soon fills up with men of all ages.

A few soldiers stand on guard at the entrance of a building while their comrades force their way in. They thoroughly search and ransack the place looking for supposed Chinese soldiers and – even more important – young women. Several homes are raided on Hankou Road. Women are raped while their men folk are forced to look on. If they protest they are shot. Those who are smart enough to keep their mouths shut still face scrutiny as Japanese soldiers search for any physical feature they believe to be characteristic of a Chinese soldier; bent fingers from firing a weapon or old scars that haven't quiet healed. Even having dark skin that has been exposed to the elements is reason for detention.

"What is happening?" asks Uncle.

"Quiet," says an old man.

"Soldier hunting," whispers a younger man.

Baba and Uncle notice a boy on board.

"He can't possibly be a soldier," whispers Baba.
"There is no sense in this."

A Japanese soldier shuts the gate of the truck and
motions a comrade to drive away.

"Where are they taking us?" someone asks.

A single machine gun fires off a round of bullets
before falling silent.

Rat-tat-tat-tat-tat-tat-tat-tat.

"They plan to annihilate us," says Baba. "They plan to kill us all."

Then a miracle.

In the distance Baba could see a familiar, foreign face. *Isn't that Fei Wu Sheng?*

Fei Wu Sheng also known as George Ashmore Fitch, was once Baba's mentor and teacher while Baba was a university student. Baba would frequently hang out with his friends at the Nanjing YMCA on Zhongshan Road on Saturday nights. Fitch was and still is the director of the YMCA.

The arrest of innocent Chinese men catches the attention of two foreigners who were originally called to inspect a rape and looting on Hankou Road. Fitch and his colleague, Professor Lewis Smythe from Nanjing University, are just leaving the home of a rape victim when they see Japanese soldiers loading bound, innocent men into the back of a truck. The two foreigners approach the Japanese commander in charge, making sure their bows are much lower than the commander so not to offend the man. None of the Japanese soldiers speak English and Fitch and Smythe do not speak Japanese. Both parties resort to speaking in simple Chinese even though Fitch, an American born and raised in Suzhou, could speak the language fluently much to the joy of the Chinese.

"Sir, what are you charging these men with?" Fitch inquires the commander.

The commander gives Fitch and Smythe a crocodile smile. "These men are soldiers," he replies.

The Americans could see that the man is lying. They see the young boy on board.

Smythe pulls Fitch aside and speaks to him in private and in English before returning to the truck.

"We know these men," says Smythe.

The commander smirks. He suspects a lie.

Fitch grabs Baba's sleeve. "I know this man. This is Tan Fu Ming. He owns a restaurant. He is a former student of mine."

The commander looks up and down at Baba. "*Zhende m*a? Really?"

"*Zhende*," Baba replies. "Really."

The commander does not take the bait so easily. "Do you have papers?"

Baba takes out of his pants pocket a wallet which holds his identity card. He shows it to the commander. The soldier nods and orders his men to release Baba.

"This man is my brother," said Baba. Uncle Tan also shows the Japanese his identity card before they untie him.

Smythe points to another man. "This man is my

gardener. His name is Wang An."

The commander asks the man if it is true. The man answers, "*zhende*."

"Do you have papers?" the commander asks Mr. Wang.

Mr. Wang is unsure how to answer. Baba nods in encouragement. Mr. Wang gives an incredulous but truthful answer. Yet, he is able to keep his emotions in check.

"My home was bombed in an air raid. I have lost everything, including my identity card."

The majority of the men in the truck nod in agreement. Many of them use to live outside the Safety Zone and have lost their homes and some of their families in the air raids. Baba and Uncle Tan are lucky that they live in the Safety Zone since the Japanese have agreed, at least on paper, not to attack it. There is no way that the commander in charge could verify the facts. Both Smythe and Fitch continue claiming captives even though they have never met some of these men. They also know that since many of these men have lost their papers mainly from the air raids, the Japanese have no way of checking the facts. They have to release these men to avoid losing face.

"Release the prisoners," the Japanese commander orders his men. A soldier opens the truck gate and the men jump out to freedom.

They are lucky this time.

Chapter Seven

"Sit down," Mama barks out an order.

"But Mama! I..." Ling protests.

"Quiet! Do you want those devils to find us and kill us?"

Ling bites her bottom lip to stifle a protest. She plops herself on the square, wooden stool in front in front of Mama and starts whimpering. Mama is about to take everything that made Ling who she is, a young girl on the verge of womanhood.

Mama takes an old cloth and wraps Ling's chest and shoulders before securing it with a clothes pin. She removes Ling's ribbons and combs out her braids. Ling weeps. Her tears drop on to the cloth protecting her dress. She tries to wipe her tears away with her hand but it is no use. The tears keep on flowing.

"It is you they are after," Mama says as she starts cutting Ling's hair with a pair of scissors.

Ling says nothing as she watches her long, shiny, black hair float to the ground. She closes her eyes tightly, wishing that she was in another world; a world better than the one she is in now.

She dreams that she could be in a world where she could wear high heels and skirts, just like the women in the movies. She dreams of becoming the Chinese Greta Garbo or Clara Bow. She envies Xue because her best friend gets to wear beautiful, silk *qipaos* and cosmetics just like Mae West.

Alas, she is just a noodle maker's daughter whose world teeters on the brink of war. Nanjing has been bombarded into submission by months of either aerial bombing or by the ground shelling of towns or villages near the city. When the Japanese army triumphantly entered the city they encountered very little resistance from the Chinese Army. Nor were there any citizens out on the street. The city was a ghost town.

Thankfully Ling's family lives in the Safety Zone. The area between Zhongshan North Road, Zhongyang Road, Zhongshan Road, and Hanzhong Road comprises the Safety Zone. This was the only part of the city that was not bombed by the Japanese.

"If you want to live you will have your hair cut and you will wear your brother's clothes."

Ling clenches her fists in protest. Yet, she whimpers and weeps in sadness. The snipping sound of Mama's scissors echoes as she silently fights to keep her girlhood.

Mama cuts Ling's hair until it is just a shag. She has left just enough hair to keep Ling's head warm. Had it been summer she would have cut all of it off making her daughter look like a Buddhist monk. Nonetheless, Ling still cries as she touches her head. She cannot even look at herself in a mirror.

Nai Nai breaks the silence as she enters the room with arms loaded with gray and black boys' clothes and shoes. She places them on the dresser right in front of Ling. Nai Nai has gone through Jun's things and dug out of his old school uniform and shoes.

"Put these on when you are done," Nai Nai orders Ling.

Ling does not open her eyes. The thought of her wearing her brother's clothes is beneath her dignity. A girl wearing boys' clothes in her mind is a sin. Wearing a disobedient brother's clothes exacerbates her embarrassment. Wearing a missing or perhaps a dead brother's clothes could bring bad luck.

Ling opens her eyes as Mama unwraps the cloth and shakes off Ling's hair. Ling stands up and grabs Jun's old shirt off the dresser. She slowly unbuttons the front of her dress and strips down to her underwear. Then she unfolds her brother's shirt and just stares at it.

"Why can't I have new clothes?" Ling protests.

"Ai yah!" Nai Nai incredulously responds to what she thought to be a selfish request. "Where do you suggest I buy new clothes, ah? Our ancient gates have been destroyed, the devils have taken over the telegraph office, and we have no trains or newspapers. We are cut off from the world! What a selfish girl! Just like your friend!"

Mama sits on the stool as Nai Nai covers Mama's shoulders with the same cloth used on Ling.

"Her name is Xue!" Ling shouts.

"Quiet!" Mama sternly whispers. "And put those clothes on before they rape you!"

Rape. Mama cannot believe she blurted out that word. Silence. Both women look at each other wondering what to do. Ling gets the cue.

"What? What is rape?"

"It's when a man forces you to sleep with him."

Mama said struggling to find the appropriate words.

Nai Nai slaps Mama on the shoulder. "Ai yah! You know nothing!" Nai Nai then resorts to hand gestures to define the word. "This is your hole," she said curving the fingers on her left hand into a cylinder. "This is a man's *niu niu*," Nai Nai extends her pointer and her index finger on her right hand. She then inserts her fingers into the cylinder before tapping her crotch twice. "Down here against your will."

Ling cringes. The foreign missionaries at her school taught her that sex should only take place in the context of marriage. For a woman to prostrate herself in front of a man, forced or not, is shameful. She quickly puts on Jun's shirt, grabs his old trousers from the dresser, slips them on and buttons them up before tightening up her waist with her brother's belt. No more protests. No more complaints. But Ling still had a lot of questions.

As she gets dressed Nai Nai proceeds to unravel Mama's bun. She takes the comb and runs it slowly through Mama's long, black hair.

"Mama. Will they rape you too?"

Mama could not think of an answer. After being embarrassed by her mother-in-law right in front of her daughter she just wished this day and this conversation would end.

"Nai Nai? Will you cut your hair too?"

"I'm old, fat, and ugly. What could they possibly want from me?"

"But Nai Nai, you're also a woman."

"I'm also old, fat, and ugly," Nai Nai repeated. "If they want me they can have me. I'm just one step closer to my grave."

Mama has had enough of this conversation. She is at the end of her tether. "Ling? Go find Xiao Jian and Ye Ye. Have them soil your face and hands."

"Yes Mama."

Chapter Eight

Ginling Women's College has been transformed from a
school housing a maximum of 200 students to a full flown
chaotic refugee camp of women and children. No adult
male refugees are allowed except for Ginling workers.
Japanese soldiers search the city for ex-Chinese soldiers
including male residents living in the Safety Zone. Men of all
ages and trades are routinely falsely accused of being
soldiers. Japanese soldiers would create trumped up
evidence for their charges; calluses on fingers or having
dark skin in their minds was proof that this man is a soldier.
To prevent gaining any unwanted attention from the
Japanese army and to protect the women and girls on
campus the college was designated a women's and
children's refugee camp. No Chinese male refugees are
allowed.

Girls are required to cut their hair to make them as
ugly and unattractive as possible. Any evidence of

womanhood was covered up or destroyed. Silk dresses are dyed black or blue or were ripped apart and used for another purpose.

Xue finds her current circumstances stifling. After being back at her school for a week and looking like a boy she is weary of wearing a dark dress, the school's winter uniform for students.

"I'm a boy in mourning clothes," she'd constantly complain to Meizhen.

Ever since they arrived Xue has always found something to complain about. On the day of their arrival Xue asked Yang Ayi who was to assign refugees to different buildings, if Xue could have her old dorm room.

"Girl, this is not the Metropolitan Hotel!" Yang Ayi scolded her. "You take what I give you!"

"I'm so sorry," Meizhen replied.

"Hooker? Teach your girl some manners! I've got all these other women to accommodate. I cannot acquiesce to your selfish daughter's request!"

"I'm so sorry," Meizhen repeated. "It will never happen again."

"Take your mother to the Music Building and Chapel. There's space for you. Next!"

"Yes, Ayi," said Xue. "Thank you."

Unfortunately there are no beds in the Music Building. All music instruments except several pianos in practice rooms have been moved. Refugees sleep on the floor. Some spread out quilts they have brought. Those who don't have any blankets sleep on the floor. Each floor is equipped with a bucket with a lid which serves as a night time toilet in case they have to use the bathroom at night. While the Music Building which also the Chapel, does have toilets the school cannot run the risk of women getting up in the middle of the night and getting raped or killed.

Soup kitchens have sprung up in various places around the school using portable stoves. The largest one has set up in the Quadrangle in front of the flag pole. Ginling workers have also brought in empty barrels for refugees to roast vegetables and potatoes.

Getting food to the campus and keeping the school clean has been a daunting task. Trucks loaded with rice and flour run the risk of being stopped and commandeered by the Japanese and getting clean water to cook or clean anything has proven impossible since the city's main pumping station has been constant target from air raids. Refugees are now reporting that there is blood in their rice.

"Yuck!" Xue winced as she gags on a mouthful of rice. "I can't eat this!"

Meizhen takes both of their bowls of rice. "Stay here," she instructs Xue. "I'll go to get edible rice."

She runs downstairs and out to the Quadrangle to stand in a long line of people waiting for their bowl of food. Many of them are also complaining about the bloody rice.

"We can't eat this!" screams one woman.

"It's unhealthy!" yells another.

Xue sits impatiently waiting for her mother to return. She looks out a second floor window and sees several girls her age roasting turnips in a barrel burning with coal. Her stomach aches for decent food and eating fresh turnips is much more appealing than bloody rice. But she needs a gimmick to get those turnips. She pulls from her battered suitcase a silk *qipao* and her mother's lipstick and powder that she stole. She puts them back in her suitcase, shuts it, and sneaks out of the Music Building into the garden behind it where the other girls are chatting and roasting turnips.

"What are you doing?" asks Xue.

"We're roasting turnips," says one girl. She sees Xue's suitcase. "You a new arrival?"

"No," Xue replies. "I'm a student here. I've been here a week. I think."

Xue has no idea how long she's been on campus. The days just seem to run together now with the city in ruins. There is no way to communicate with the outside world other than smuggling information out. The only way to count the days is to watch the sun and the moon rise and set, except that it is now winter and the ground is wet from melting snow.

"What's in your bag?" asks another girl.

Xue sets her suitcase down on the ground and slowly unbuckles it. "I have girl clothes and make-up," she replies. "Want to have a look?"

"Yes!" both girls enthusiastically reply.

Xue opens her suitcase. The girls, who also had their hair cut and are now wearing black dresses like Xue, ooh and ahh over her *qipao* and cosmetics.

"*Hen piaoliang!*" exclaims the first girl as she takes the *qipao.*

"Who are you and where did you get these things?" asks the second girl.

"Xue."

"Lijuan."

"Anping."

Xue is relieved that these girls have no idea who she is. Refugees from the villages and towns surrounding Nanjing are flowing in hoping to find a better situation only to find out that Nanjing is in no better condition than the conditions in their hometowns.

"My mother is a hotel worker," Xue replies careful not to reveal Meizhen's true occupation. "She serves foreign guests."

"I've always wanted to wear dresses like this," says Anping.

Lijuan takes out some of the cosmetics. "Just like the poster girls! I'm so tired of wearing this ugly dress!" she complains.

"How about a trade?" Xue suggests. "I can let you wear my *qipao* and help you with your make-up and you give me some of your turnips?"

"Deal!" the other two girls shout in unison.

"But there's only one *qipao*," says Lijuan.

"We can take turns," says Anping.

"I should go first so that you can watch and learn how

to put it on and how to paint your face," says Xue.

Chapter Nine

Minnie Vautrin is on guard at the gatehouse of Ginling Women's College. She stands outside at the main gate. Ever since the fall most of her days are spent at the gate monitoring the situation or investigating an intrusion by Japanese soldiers. She hardly has a moment to herself. She can't even finish a meal without a servant interrupting her. Earlier today she was called to investigate a possible intrusion. A light in a teacher's residence was left on.

It was a false alarm. Her fellow westerners Minor Searle Bates and Charles Henry Riggs had turned it on the night before and forgot to turn it off.

All day women endlessly stream into the college with ashen and dreary faces. Many have endured enemy soldiers breaking into their homes in the middle of the night killing their men and raping their women. Many tell of how there were gang raped in front of family members. Others tell of how Japanese soldiers forced their husbands and sons to rape the female members of their families. If the men refused they were killed and the soldiers would rape the women.

"My mother was raped and killed before my eyes," cried a woman.

"They yanked my nursing baby out of my arms and smashed his head on the floor!" wailed another.

"I awoke to find my daughter tied to a chair violated and dead!"

Oh how I wish all of these stories could be recorded Minnie thought as these poor women passed through the gate.

There are just too many to listen to. Yet the theme is all the same. Every family has endured a night of torture and mayhem. But it is the women of Nanjing who have suffered the most.

The Tan family is fortunate that Baba and Uncle Tan were released due to members of the International Safety Zone Committee negotiating with the Japanese. But they are still missing their fifteen year old son Jun whom they fear, has run away presumably to join the Chinese army.

But which army did he join? The local militia? Or the Guomindang?

There was also the possibility he could have been abducted by the Japanese. They have no idea where Jun could be.

Ling, Mama, and Nai Nai have come to Ginling Women's College looking for an answer to their question. Rumor has it that Minnie Vautrin could locate missing relatives. They wanted to know if the rumor is true. Making a phone call is now impossible city lines are down. The only way they could make an inquiry is in person.

Walking to the college is quite risky. Although they live in the Safety Zone and are within walking distance at the school's main gate, Japanese soldiers are everywhere some are in plain sight. Others are inside looting or raping women.

Young women are easily lured to their deaths with gifts. A soldier approaches a girl and comments on her beauty.

"Such a pretty girl," they say in broken Chinese using such sweet talk to woo the ladies. Girls are innocently lured by candy, perfumes, combs, or some other gift. Soldiers would claim they have more of these items and they would be willing to give them to the girls if they would just follow the soldiers. But more experienced women would swiftly meet their demise if they resisted.

"I won't follow you," says one street wise woman. "I'm already married and have children."

Enraged by her refusal the soldier runs a bayonet through her body, rips off her clothing, and proceeds to rape the now dying woman on the street.

Homes they pass on their way to school displays evidence of an intrusion and rape. Some doors are open.

Others have doors that have been kicked or rammed down. Sometimes a soldier stands guard at the entrance while his comrades take turns raping a woman. Occasional screams could be heard from the building. Women could be seen naked on the street sitting on the sidewalk while soldiers take photos of their conquests.

Mama and Nai Nai take great pains to avert Ling's attention. They make her look the other way or stare at the ground as they walk. They would have liked for her to stay home with the men and Aunty Shen but since she knows the campus and Minnie they have no choice but to take her. Many of these women are neighbors who would have liked to verbally warn the family but restrained themselves for fear of exposing Ling even though she is dressed as a boy.

It is approaching dusk. As they get closer to campus the streets of Hankou, West Hankou, and Ninghai Road are teaming with refugees mainly women and girls struggling to get to the school gate before sundown. Many have endured sleepless nights. Many just want a place of safety from roaming Japanese soldiers who barge in their homes in the darkness and just start raping and killing at will.

The Tan family have to compete with all these women for Minnie's attention. Minnie and her Chinese colleague,

Dr. Blanche Wu, are seen at the main gate comforting women and girls.

"Miss Vautrin! Dr. Wu!" Ling shouts in English.

"Tan Ling?" says Dr. Wu. "Is that you?"

"I almost didn't recognize you," said Minnie. "What can we do for you?"

"My brother, Jun, is gone. We want to know if you can help us find him."

Minnie confers with Dr. Wu while Ling translates for Mama and Nai Nai.

"Come inside," Minnie encouraged all of them to talk confidentially in the gate house. "When was the list time you saw him?"

"It's been a month since he ran away," said Mama.

"Ran away?" asked Dr. Wu. "Why?"

"He wanted to join the army," Ling replied. "But my father refused to let him go."

"He just left," said Nai Nai. "We took him to school on a Sunday. We expected he'd return on Friday as usual."

"But he didn't return home," Mama further explained.

"Do you know which army?" Minnie asked Ling.

"No."

"Do you have a photo of him?" asked Dr. Wu.

"Yes, we do." Ling takes out of her pocket Jun's school I.D. photo. Minnie takes the photo and hands it to her colleague.

"Have you tried contacting the Government Office?" asked Dr. Wu.

"Dr. Wu," said Mama, "my husband and his brother would go to the Guomindang Headquarters. But they nearly lost their lives the other day. They were saved by two foreign men who negotiated their freedom."

"Why are you asking about which army Jun joined?" Nai Nai wanted to know.

"If he joined the local militia there's still a chance he may still be in the city," Dr. Wu replied. "But if he joined the Guomindang Army he could be anywhere between Nanjing and Chongqing by now. That is, if he is still alive."

"Only General Tang would know," Minnie chimed in. "I'll see what I can do. May I keep your brother's picture?" she asks Ling.

"Yes. Thank you."

Just then a tall, burly Chinese man rushes into the gatehouse. He staggers and nearly falls and gasps as he tries to speak.

"Miss Vautrin!" the man pants.

"What is it Big Wang?"

"Three girls are missing from the Music Building. One of..."

Big Wang recognizes Ling, a former student of his, in her disguise. He slowly inhales several times to compose himself and gather his thoughts.

"Maybe we should talk outside."

Minnie excuses herself as the Tan family prepare to leave and head home before the night time curfew. She and Dr. Wu step outside to have a private conversation with Big Wang.

"What is it?" Dr. Wu asks.

"One of the missing girls is Xue," says Big Wang. "Her mother is screaming and crying for her girl."

"Where is she?" asks Minnie.

"The mother is in the Music Building."

"You go, Minnie," Dr. Wu suggests. "I'll stay at the gate."

Just outside the gate a truck loaded with ten women and girls in the back drives by as the Tans are about to cross the street. Young women and girls with arms outstretched scream for help at the top of their lungs.

"*Jiu ming! Jiu ming!*" they all cry.

Ling spots a familiar face in the truck. Xue is kneeling with one hand outstretched. Her pain ridden face is covered with powder and lipstick. Her new found friends Anping and

Lijuan are also in the truck bed pleading for their lives. Lijuan is also wearing Xue's *qipao*.

"Xue?"

"Ling?" Xue sees her best friend on the street as the truck rumbles on. *"Jiu ming! Jiu ming!"* she screams in desperation as she tries to reach for Ling's outstretched hand.

"Jump Xue! Jump!" Ling screams as she chases after the fast moving vehicle.

"Ai ya!" Mama screams as she and Nai Nai run after Ling in a vain attempt to conceal her true gender. "That girl!"

"Jiu ming! Jiu ming!" Xue and the others in the truck yell as Minnie, Dr. Wu, and Big Wang helplessly watch.

Ling is hysterically crying as she is running after the truck. "Xue!" she wails. She eventually stops and drops to her knees as she can no longer keep up with her friend. She sobs uncontrollably as Mama and Nai Nai try to get Ling back on her feet.

They cannot linger much longer. They must get home. The night time curfew is fast approaching and another night of hell is about to fall on the beleaguered women of Nanjing.

Chapter Ten

Baba anxiously waits for the three women and his brother to return. He constantly steps outside on the sidewalk to see if they are on their way. His heart rate increases as the curfew approaches. Ginling Women's College and Uncle Tan's Red Swastika Society[2] meeting are both on Ninghai Road within walking distance from West Hankou Road but they might as well be on the moon.

---

[2] The Red Swastika Society is an organization similar to the Red Cross. Although they have a swastika as a symbol they have no connection to the Nazi Party. Their swastika is 卐 as opposed to the Nazi symbol which looks like this 卍.

The women arrive in time to assist Baba, Ye Ye, Aunty Shen, and Ling's two younger brothers Xiao Jian and Xiao Wei to shut down their restaurant which has since been converted to a community soup kitchen. The bowls have to washed and dried. The woks need a good scrubbing. The coals must be extinguished and tables must be wiped.

However, Ling is too furious to assist her family. She immediately runs upstairs and barricades herself in her room.

"What happened?" Baba asks.

"She ran after a truck screaming her head off," says Nai Nai.

"She saw her friend in the truck," replied Mama.

"The prostitute's daughter?" asks Ye Ye.

"Yes," Mama replies solemnly.

Baba senses the danger in the air. By screaming and chasing down her friend Ling may have inadvertently revealed her true gender. He is glad that she is home. But where is his brother? After experiencing their own encounter with the Japanese soldiers the other day he would have learned by now to not be out at this time of night.

"We will spend the night in the cellar," says Baba.

"Dinner is ready," Aunty Shen announces.

"I'll get Ling," says Mama as she walks upstairs to get her daughter. She knocks on the door but there is no response. She wasn't expecting any. "You can come down when you are ready."

Ten minutes later Ling arrives at the table. She eats but says nothing. No one speaks. Everyone is silent. Only the clatter of chopsticks and bowls could be heard as the family eats a simple meal of rice and pickled vegetables.

Jian breaks the silence. "I'm tired of eating bloody

rice!"

"Quiet!" says Baba.

"Just eat your vegetables then," says Mama as she dollops more vegetables in the boy's rice bowl.

There is a loud knock at the restaurant gate.

"To the cellar," Baba orders everyone to take cover. Mama, Nai Nai, Aunty Shen, gather the children and they head to the back of the restaurant kitchen and walk down one flight of stairs to the restaurant cellar.

"Boys!" Mama whispers to Xiao Jian and Xiao Wei. "Quietly!"

The boys quietly put down their bowls and chopsticks and follow the women while Baba and Ye Ye slowly unlock the gate hoping all the while that the person knocking is Uncle Tan.

"Good evening kind sir," says a smiling Japanese soldier in broken Chinese with his bayonet fixed on his rifle.

Baba could see that there were at least nine other soldiers standing behind him on the street.

"*Mi fan arimasuka?*" the soldier asks him.

Do you have any rice?

"We are closed," Baba and Ye Ye reply.

From the cellar the family hears two shots fired. Mama and Nai Nai shutter upon hearing them go off. They hear their loved ones slump to the floor. They hear footsteps in the dining area where the family was eating just minutes ago. They hear the clattering of bowls and chopsticks.

They hear a strange language.

"*Yaku! Chimamire no gohan!*" yells one soldier.

Yuck! Bloody rice.

"Shikashi, yasai wa daijobudesu."

But the vegetables are okay," says another as he devours some of the food.

Some of the soldiers search the kitchen. They overturn the portable stoves and dump out the remaining coal before placing it in a large burlap sack.

Then one of them discovers the staircase leading to the cellar.

"Lieutenant Sasaki," he calls out to his leader.

Lieutenant Sasaki, the soldier who speaks Chinese, enters the kitchen. The door to the cellar is closed.

"Open it," Sasaki orders one of his men.

"It's locked, sir."

Sasaki signals another soldier to assist. "Break it down," he barks out the order.

Several soldiers break down the wooden door first with the butt of their bayonets and then breaking through by kicking a hole in the door. One of them sticks his hand in and opens the door from inside.

The women and children have no where else to go. They are trapped.

"Dansei. Anata no hoshu ga arimasu," says the lieutenant.

Boys. There is your reward.

The women are huddled in the farthest corner of the cellar protecting Ling, Xiao Jian, and Xiao Wei.

Nai Nai is first. One soldier grabs her by the collar and throws her on the ground. Nai Nai lands on her back. Aunty Shen rushes over to Nai Nai to protect her but she is brutally hit in the head with a rifle butt. She is knocked unconscious. Mama and Ling and the boys try to run to their rescue but they are forced back into their corner by at least five other soldiers with their bayonets pointed at the family.

"Mother!" Mama screams.

"Nai Nai!" Ling and her brothers call out.

The lieutenant barks out an order to his men. *"Naite iru sugi no buta wa anata no tsugi no gisei-shadesu."*

The next pig that squeals is your next victim.

"You don't want me!" yells Nai Nai. "I'm an old woman."

But the soldier fails to hear her. With one swift blow of the butt of his bayonet he hits the old woman's forehead before taking off her jacket and her pants. Blood trickles out of Nai Nai's mouth as she breathes her last breath.

Then the soldier unfastens his belt and drops his pants.

"Ling! Boys! Close your eyes!" Mama instructs them. They try to obey but two soldiers lay their tips of their bayonets blades on their cheeks forcing the family to watch as their comrade assaults Nai Nai before stabbing her with his weapon.

Aunty Shen fares much worse treatment. A soldier slices open her belly thus exposing her unborn child. Then another soldier cuts the umbilical chord and slices the baby in half with his katana as if the embryo were a sausage. There is blood everywhere. Just as they did with Nai Nai they proceed to take off their victim's clothes before taking off theirs and raping a dying Aunty Shen.

A soldier spots a broom stick in the cellar and gives it to his naked colleague who shoves it up Aunty Shen's vagina.

"*Seiseidesu. Kanajo wa kasshite futatabi ninshin suru koto wa dekimasen,*" he jokes to his comrades.

Purification. She can never get pregnant again!

The soldiers laugh as Ling and Mama watch the horror happening in front of them. Some of the soldiers take turns raping Nai Nai and Aunty Shen.

Then Xiao Jian breaks free from the family to tries to run to Nai Nai but a soldier shoots him in the back with a pistol. The boy quickly falls over into a pool of blood.

Mama holds Xiao Wei tightly to her chest. But a half naked soldier pries him from her arms. He then tosses the toddler into the air where his comrade thrusts his bayonet into the child skewering him like barbequed meat. The soldier then takes the tiny carcass, slides it off the blade with his boot, picks it up and tosses it into the stair case. By doing so the boy's head smashes against the wall.

Mama is horrified. To see two of her offspring killed in an instant she becomes weak in her knees and falls to the ground.

"Mama!" Ling cries. "Get up! Get up!"

Lieutenant Sasaki recognizes the girl. By now all of his men are naked or at least have no pants on. Only Sasaki is clothed.

"Ahh!" he says to Ling. *"Otokonoko no yo ni doresu o suru shojo."* He laughs.

The girl who dresses like a boy.

"Soretomo shojo no yo ni kodo suru shonendesu ka?" he continues.

Or is it the boy who acts like a girl?

Ling stops screaming for a moment at the lieutenant touches her cheek. She struggles to break free but is held back by two men.

"Watashi wa kanojo o saisho ni gokan suru," says Sasaki as he unbuttons his pants. *"Watashi wa kanojo ga*

ikite hoshi."

I get her first. I want her alive.

The two soldiers holding Ling back throw her to the ground. She screams as the soldiers pin her arms to the floor with their knees. One of them slaps Ling hard on the face with his hand.

She loses all consciousness. She feels and remembers no more.

Chapter Eleven

Uncle Tan sits in his relief truck behind the wheel at the Japanese Embassy with several other Red Swastika volunteers. They are all waiting for Rabe to leave the Embassy so that they can return safely to their families in the Zone. Uncle Tan wishes he could be with his wife and assist his brother in the running of their restaurant which has been converted into a soup kitchen run by the Red Swastika Society.

But Nanjing is in need of basic services including street cleaning and sanitation. A part of that includes the disposing of mounds of decaying flesh lying on the streets left by rampaging Japanese soldiers. This daunting task has been left to several burial societies who depend on volunteers. The largest and most well known one is the Red Swastika Society.

That pool of volunteers however, keeps shrinking as Japanese troops keep taking men away to be killed. The Society's work has also been thwarted by the fact that the Japanese have made it illegal to dispose of corpses. Soldiers also continuously commandeer relief trucks at makeshift checkpoints around the city.

The events from two days ago remain fresh in Uncle Tan's mind. He and his team of volunteers are given their orders by Mr. Xiang, president of the Nanjing chapter of the Society, and by Smythe, from Nanjing University. They are to leave the Safety Zone and dispose of bodies from Xiaguan District to the junction where North Zhongshan, Zhonyang, and Zhongshan Roads meet. Twenty-five men show up to receive their orders and vehicles. They are divided into teams of six or seven and given the area where they are to clear of corpses. Smythe is to oversee the operation and to survey the city.

The convoy of four trucks turn north on North Zhongshan Road heading to the harbor and train station. Bodies litter the streets both inside and outside the Zone. They immediately encounter a makeshift checkpoint guarded by Japanese soldiers who hold up traffic. Smythe, who is in the last vehicle with Uncle Tan at the wheel, clenches his fist and starts cursing in English before getting out. Uncle and the men in his truck also attempt to get out but Smythe raises his hand to stop them.

Several soldiers forcibly open all four trucks and force the men out at gunpoint. Red Swastika volunteers exit the cabs and jump off truck beds with their hands in the air or on their heads.

"What is going on?" Smythe shouts. "Who is in command here?"

He gets no response as the soldiers continue to force volunteers, including those in Smythe's truck, out of their vehicle at gunpoint. Some of the soldiers point their weapons at the volunteers while their comrades search them for weapons and keys to their trucks. One soldier confiscates a baton and presents it to Smythe.

"A stick?" the soldier asks in heavily accented English.

"Some of these men are also volunteer police for the Safety Zone," Smythe explains. "They are allowed batons but no guns."

The soldier smiles. Then he laughs and issues orders in Japanese. "Tie them up and load them into *their* trucks."

A few soldiers retrieve coils of rope and start tying volunteers up as if they are common criminals.

"They are with me!" Smythe continues to protest. But the Japanese refuse to listen and continue to hold Riggs at gunpoint while their comrades continue to tie up volunteers. Eventually they run out of rope.

"No more rope!" shouts a soldier.

Fourteen men are tied while the rest, including Uncle Tan, are forced to watch at gunpoint. The volunteers then jump in the back of their trucks now commandeered by Japanese troops. They leave willingly without complaining.

"What shall we do with the remaining policemen?" asks a soldier.

"Kill them," his commander replies. "Kill them all."

But Smythe stands resolutely between the remaining volunteers and enemy guns. "If you shoot them, you'll have to shoot me first."

Meanwhile Japanese soldiers have attempted to commandeer Riggs' truck. Soldiers are jumping into the cab and on to the bed. While the previous three trucks were to be used to transport victims to be killed, Smythe's truck was for their own personal use.

"And you are not taking my truck," Smythe continues. The soldiers laugh.

"Very well," their leader releases them with a smug face. "You may have your truck." He then orders his men out of the last truck. Some of them return to man their checkpoint while others jump into the cabs or beds of the vehicles they just commandeered.

Smythe takes command of the volunteers. "*Yaoshi*?" He asks Uncle Tan who then hands over the keys to the vehicle. Smythe and the volunteers promptly return to the International Safety Zone Committee Headquarters to report the incident to Rabe who then writes a letter to Kiyoshi Fukui, Second Secretary to the Japanese Embassy, outlining the incident.

They were unable to dispose of any corpses that day.

Chapter Twelve

No one seems to have any sense of time. The days just seem to run together non-stop. There are fires in different parts of the city. Munitions depots explode. Looted homes outside the Zone are set ablaze. The smell of decaying bodies is mixed in with smoke and gunpowder is suffocating.

It is dark. Uncle Tan guesses it's around 11 p.m. Rabe and George Rosen, a diplomat from the German Embassy emerge from the Japanese Embassy compound bowing to Fukui before getting into the truck. Both men look haggard from hours of negotiations with the Japanese and also conducting multiple tours and patrols in and outside the Zone.

Uncle Tan and his fellow volunteers are just as tired. In addition to digging mass burial sites they also truck in food to various refugee camps inside the Zone and operate soup kitchens.

They have yet to bury a single body. Every day more and more corpses are added to the heaps of bodies on the streets. Every day workers are thwarted by the Japanese authorities and soldiers on the ground running wild and uncontrolled. This beastly behavior has caused widespread panic especially among the women. Many of them seek refuge in American run institutions such as Ginling Women's College and Nanjing University. Two prospective refugee shelters are completely empty due to soldiers constantly taking the men away for slaughter, leaving the women no choice but to seek refuge and another shelter, preferably one where there is a westerner present.

Your searching squads have cleaned out all of them and many civilians along with them Rabe writes in a second letter to Secretary Fukui outlining their demands for the Japanese for better protection of civilians and better control over their soldiers.

Rosen jumps in the truck bed with the volunteers who are struggling to stay awake while Rabe gets into the cab.

"Zou ba!" Rabe instructs Uncle Tan.

Let's go.

They drop off volunteers at various refugee camps inside the Zone. Bodies of victims are strewn out on the streets left to freeze in the winter cold. The Safety Zone is safe in name only. It is anything but safe. Yet it's much safer than the mayhem happening outside the Zone. Structures are on fire. Businesses have been looted. At least the Zone offers victims some shelter as there has been only minor damage to buildings inside the Zone.

Uncle Tan turns on to Hankou Road, the final stretch to his home. He is the last volunteer to be dropped off before the Germans return to the International Safety Zone Headquarters to turn the night watch over to another pair of westerners.

An ominous single light is left on and the gate to the restaurant is wide open. The three men proceed to enter cautiously with Uncle Tan leading the way and Rabe holding his lantern. Uncle falls to his knees in shock. Baba and Ye Ye's bodies lay before him. Their blood is fresh but their spirits are already gone.

They hear voices inside the home. Uncle Tan points to

the ground beneath him. He gets back on his feet and leads the two Germans quietly to the cellar. Uncle Tan nearly stumbles over the crumpled body of a child. He and the Germans by now have gotten used to seeing human body parts gutted out and left to rot.

Is it Xiao Jian? Uncle thinks to himself. *Or is it Xiao Wei?*

The door to the cellar is still open and Lieutenant Sasaki and his men are still there. All are either naked or half dressed. One of them is sitting on Ling.

Rabe now takes charge of the situation. By now he has gotten used to recuing victims. He grabs Ling's rapist by the arm, yanks him off his victim, and thrusts his Nazi armband in the soldier's face.

"Do you see this?" Rabe shouts causing the half naked soldier's ear to ring from Rabe's screaming. He shutters and nods yes.

"I'm German! *Deutche!* Germany! Japan! Friends!"

The lieutenant and his men flee. Ling's rapist can only grab his trousers and runs half naked with his fellow soldiers.

Rabe checks Ling for a pulse while Rosen and Uncle Tan wrap her in Uncle's jacket.

"She's still alive!"

Rosen translates for Uncle Tan who quickly scoops her into his arms and carries her.

"Quick! Let's get her to Robert!" says Rosen.

The three men carry Ling up the stairs through the kitchen and dining area to their truck which is still there.

They have no time to check on anyone else in the home. All are dead.

Uncle Tan places Ling in the bed. He and Rosen ride in

the back while Rabe drives frantically to Gulou Hospital. All the while Uncle cradles Ling's head in his lap.

"I'm so sorry my dear Ling!" he cries repeatedly. "If only I had come home earlier. Then this wouldn't have happened."

"Don't be too hard on yourself," says Rosen.

The truck lurches to a streaking stop at Gulou Hospital's emergency room. The hospital grounds are covered with refugees and camps. Refugees are wide awake despite the late night hour and fearfully they ask the mostly male hospital staff what is happening.

Rabe, as tired as he is, gets out to investigate while Rosen assists Uncle Tan in unloading Ling. Among the staff is the only operating surgeon in Nanking, Dr. Robert Wilson.

"Sorry about this, John," a weary Wilson apologizes. "We've had several intrusions about two hours ago." He glances at Ling. "Take her to the top floor," he orders Uncle Tan in fluent Nanjing dialect.

Uncle carries Ling to the top floor with the assistance of several hospital staff while Rabe and Rosen investigate the intrusions with Dr. Wilson. As Uncle Tan carries Ling up several hospital workers are busy moving patients up and down stairs. The result is chaos.

"What happened, Robert?"

"Three Jap soldiers tramped up and down our hallways. Miss Hynd bumped into them on her rounds. They took watches, including Miss Hynd's as well as several fountain pens. Two of them departed. But the third just disappeared."

"When was that?" asks Rosen.

"Around eight," Wilson continues. "Then around nine fifteen I found three Japs in the nurses' dormitory. One of them was raping one of my nurses. I'm ordering all women, both female patients and nurses, to the top three floors of the hospital for safety reasons"

"Did you request a guard or a police force?" asks Rabe.

"We're a hospital. Didn't think we'd need a guard. But now I'll have to put in a request with the Japanese Embassy for one."

"Do you have any other committee members helping you?" says Rabe.

"Trimmer is out of commission. He can't help with the surgeries. But he's here doing what he can. Reverend Magee is also here with his camera. And, of course Miss Hynd."

"Good," Rabe replies. "Keep up the good work."

Rabe and Rosen get into their truck and return to the Safety Zone Headquarters for a changing of the guard and some much needed rest.

Chapter Thirteen

Minnie Vautrin is engaged in a stand off in her office. Her opponent is Major Nomura, a man of small stature who musters every bit of stoicism to face this formidable woman. Although it is Christmas Eve morning, Minnie is in no mood to exchange warm Christmas greetings with the enemy.

Ever since the fall of the city on December 13th, Japanese soldiers have barged in on the campus almost daily. The campus is now home to nearly 10,000 refugees. Every inch of open space including the Quadrangle, is occupied. The once green grasses of that lawn is now become a muddied refugee camp. Refugees slosh their way through.

Standing between the two adversaries is Minnie's desk and Mr. Luo, an elderly Chinese translator who works for the Japanese Embassy.

"Major Nomura is requesting one hundred women for a licensed brothel."

Minnie is incredulous. She cannot believe that this old man would sell out his country to the enemy.

Mr. Luo continues in English. "He believes that if he's given one hundred women his men will stop molesting innocent and decent women."

Exactly one week prior to this stand off a day after Xue and her new friends were taken, a servant boy runs to the main gate to report another intrusion. "Miss Vautrin! Enemy soldiers are heading to the dormitories!"

Again? Minnie thinks to herself. *Didn't we just go through this yesterday?*

All of Minnie's days just seem to run together. Every day there seems to be an incursion. She just runs from one crisis to another. She chases soldiers back over the school wall. She's called to investigate a possible rape. She's needed at the gate to prevent soldiers from entering. The school does have a small police force. But they are not enough to deter any intruder. Since they have no weapons do to the International Safety Zone bylaws all they can do is report the incursion to a westerner.

Minnie and the boy rush to the dormitories along with Mr. Li, Ginling's assistant business manager to investigate the incursion. On the way they find two Japanese soldiers pulling on the door to the Central Building.

"Open!"

"I have no key!" says Minnie.

"Soldiers here!" yells one soldier in broken English. "Enemy of Japan!"

"No Chinese soldiers here!"

"Yes," said Mr. Li. "No soldiers here."

The soldiers are displeased with both of their responses. One of them slaps Minnie in the face with his hand. But with Mr. Li he slaps him even harder causing Mr. Li's lip to bleed. He coolly wipes the blood off with his hand. Mr. Li is stunned but like most Nanjing-ren he is getting use to the atrocities.

"Open it!" the other soldier demanded.

"I don't have the key!" Minnie repeats. "But there is another entrance." She and Mr. Li then lead the soldiers into the building. Both men thoroughly search upstairs and downstairs in every office, including Minnie's, in the reception area, beneath every desk and in every closet for Chinese soldiers. As they leave the Central Building two more soldiers come with three of Ginling's servants all bound with ropes.

"Chinese soldiers!"

Minnie and Mr. Li grab all three captives by their arms. "No! Not soldiers!" Minnie screams. "Coolie! Gardener!"

But the soldiers refuse to release their victims and take them back to the main gate. Minnie and Mr. Li follow. When they get there they are dismayed to find several of their colleagues, including Mr. Li's boss, Francis Chen, and several servants, including Yang Ayi, kneeling on the sidewalk. Some have their hands on their heads while others are kowtowing to the soldiers.

Leading this search operation is Sergeant Ota. "Who is in charge here?" he asks.

Minnie steps forward. "I am."

"Identify these people. If you can identify them correctly we will release them."

The pressure is on Minnie to correctly identify everyone. Some of them she knows personally like Francis and Yang Ayi. There are others, however, that are new to her that were hired as extra help. Minnie has no idea if these people have their I.D. cards on them or if the Japanese have already confiscated them.

Francis tries to intervene on Minnie's behalf. "She's an American!" he protests. A soldier slaps him in the face, grabs him by the arm, drags him across the street and forces him to kneel. Minnie and Mr. Li fear that will be the last time they will see of him.

Just then a car pulls up in front of the gate. Fitch, Smythe, and Mills exit the vehicle. Soldiers force the three American men to stand in line and remove their hats. They comply without complaint.

"Search them!" Ota orders his men.

The sergeant's men search the Americans for weapons mainly pistols. The two items that members of the International Safety Zone Committee promised not to allow into the Zone are uniformed Chinese soldiers and weapons. While the Japanese have not recognized the Zone, they have at least allowed it to exist. Therefore the Americans have come clean and have no weapons.

"All you foreigners must leave. Now!" Ota orders. He points his pistol at Smythe. All three men raise their hands and kneel to keep the peace. They know better than to anger any Japanese.

Then Ota turns his weapon on Minnie. She struggles to collect her thoughts as she stares down the barrel of a gun. She gets on her knees and kowtows. "This school *is* my home, sir. I cannot leave!"

Ota pauses. "Very well. You can stay." Then he points his gun at Mills. "But you three must leave. Now!"

Suddenly they hear a chorus of women and girls screaming and rushing out another nearby gate. Minnie and her fellow Americans soon realize that this mock search for Chinese soldiers and weapons was a trick to get what the Japanese really wanted. Women. One group of soldiers would distract responsible people while another group would kidnap women and girls.

Minnie is crestfallen. She has been charged with looking after these people. It is one thing to kidnap victims behind her back and to investigate the crime after it has happened. But it's even more discouraging when the kidnapping happens just under her nose and there is nothing she can do about it but pray.

I have failed them.

"You can tell your Major Nomura I will only acquiesce to his request if he and his men will truly keep their word and not take innocent and decent women," Minnie replies with a stern face.

Mr. Luo translates for the major. He stands and bows his head as a way to thank Minnie before they all leave her office and stand on the balcony overlooking the reception area. Japanese soldiers have rounded up women of all ages into the hall. Many are quite nervous and look tired as they have endured several sleepless nights of intrusion and kidnappings.

Minnie would like to speak to these women in Chinese but she is tired of having to think in English before searching her exhausted brain to find the appropriate words in Chinese. "Mr. Luo? *Fayin!*"

Mr. Luo steps forward to Minnie's left to translate while Major Nomura flanks her right. The women look at the major with fear and apprehension.

"I'm a virgin," one girl whispers. "Are they going to take me?"

Minnie speaks. "It is with great reservation that I have to make this request of you women." She looks at the major. "The major needs one hundred prostitutes to operate a licensed brothel. He has also promised not to take any young girls and decent women." She nods at the major who then issues an order to his men before returning to Minnie's office. As the soldiers search for prostitutes the women are put on edge.

"Ladies, please!" says Minnie in a desperate attempt to calm them down. "They only want prostitutes. If you are decent they will not harm you!"

The crowd calms down but their anxiety is still present.

Finally Meizhen steps forward. Although she is now dressed in black to mourn the loss of her daughter and her hair is no longer coiffed, she can't seem to escape her lot in life, to be a sexual slave to men.

"C'mon ladies. We've got clients to entertain."

Slowly some of Meizhen's friends and colleagues from

the Metropolitan Hotel as well as other Nanjing hotels and brothels in the Qinhuai River area, step forward. The soldiers secure twenty-one courtesans from the crowd. Minnie is shocked. She never expected to find these women in her refugee camp.

The courtesans leave followed by the soldiers. Mr. Luo informs the major who is sitting in Minnie's office that the women have left. As the translator and the major leave her office, Minnie expresses her contempt to Mr. Luo.

"*Pantu*," she utters in Chinese before switching to English. *Traitor.* "You should be ashamed of yourself."

Meanwhile the remaining women are still apprehensive and start talking among themselves.

"If they can take twenty-one ladies now, what's to stop them from taking more later on?"

"What's the chance that they will take innocent and decent girls?"

Minnie tries to calm their fears as she walks down to comfort them.

"Will they come back?" asks one woman.

"They said they want one hundred. But they only got twenty-one," says another woman. "What's to stop them from returning and picking out the remaining seventy-nine from decent and innocent girls?"

Minnie digs deep within herself to be resolute and to stop herself from weeping for those women who have volunteered. Yet she is also seething with anger. "They won't," she says with a clinched fist and a defiant voice. "They will not do so if it is my power to prevent it."

Chapter Fourteen

Date. Unknown. Time. Unknown.

The days just seem to blend together. There are no clocks or watches. There are no calendars except those in heaps of rubbish strewn all over the streets of Nanjing. The only way to tell the passage of time is through the seasons and through notices put up by the Japanese authorities.

Snow continues to fall. There are no children to create snowmen or have snowball fights. Indeed there is no one. They are all dead. As Dr. Wilson writes:

The year is fast drawing to a close. It would be pleasant to close the year with some sort of brighter outlook for the next but we seem to be closing on a note of deepest gloom without a glimmer of light ahead. The only consolation is that it can't get any worse. They can't kill as many people as there aren't any more to kill.

A thin layer of ice covers Xuanwu Lake and the Yangtze River. They crack with the slightest movement. Bodies pile up on the banks of the Yangtze. Red Swastika volunteers and other burial organizations in the area are given the gruesome task of burning corpses along the river.

The river bleeds blood.

Why me? Uncle Tan has had no time to mourn his loss. *Why them and not me? If I had been home none of this would have happened.*

Today is the first day the Red Swastika Team is allowed to clear the streets. They are assigned the northwest quadrant of the city from Xiaguan District to North Zhongshan Road. Uncle Tan and his team leave the Safety Zone Headquarters with their swastika armbands tied to their arms. The team certainly cannot always expect a westerner to accompany them for the twenty something foreigners are already stretched thin. The western men sleep at Ginling Women's College or Nanjing University where only female refugees are accepted. Others act as policemen running from one crisis to another and conducting patrols of the Zone. Then there are western doctors like Wilson who cannot leave the hospital for they are inundated with victims in need of care. Uncle Tan and his team can only hope that their swastika would act as a deterrent.

"Let's hope those devils can't tell the difference."

After turning their truck onto North Zhonshan Road they encounter a fence entangled with barbed wire. The head of a man sits on that fence and there is a cigarette dangling from his mouth. Across the street and outside of the Zone are rows of heads both male and female all neatly lined up against a bombed out building. There are also bodies scattered every few hundred yards. Some are piled up on top of each other. The smell of decomposing bodies is nauseating and some of the men cover their noses and mouths with whatever cloth they can find while others just endure the smell.

As Uncle and his crew jump out of their truck to clear the road block he steps on an old newspaper article. He can't read the Japanese writing on it. However, from the Chinese characters he understands the story behind it. It infuriates him.

"Look at this," Uncle Tan shows the article to his comrades.

The article features a photo of two Japanese lieutenants named Toshiaki Mukai and Tsuyoshi Noda. The headline reads:

Incredible Record in the Contest to Cut Down 100 People! Mukai 106! Noda 105!

"*Se lang!*" Uncle mutters out loud. His men don't understand.

"Sex maniacs?" one of them asks clearly confused.

"No. Beasts. Predators. They kill our men and rape our women. Every one of them deserves hell. They killed my wife and unborn child. They smashed my two nephews' brains and skewered one like a meat stick. They shot my brother and father…"

Some of the men are clearly distressed at Uncle's remarks for they have gone through the same thing.

"Sorry. Let's get to work."

It is difficult to make friends in this environment. What is the point of calling each other by name if that name will soon be just a body? What is the point of consoling each other when you really don't know each other? Uncle Tan has no idea who these men are or where they are from. They have seen their comrades kidnapped by the enemy and have no idea if they will be next. They fear starting friendships because the pain of loss is already excruciating. All of these volunteers have lost family in one way or another.

But the thing that infuriates them the most is the way the enemy treats the women of Nanjing. Some of these men were forced to watch their mothers and daughters suffer. Some were forced to rape their own family members under duress. There is nothing more painful than hearing the screams of a *nai nai*. There is nothing more excruciating than watching a daughter being raped and killed right before your eyes. Out of all the people that have suffered it is the women of Nanjing who bear the brunt of the atrocities.

The men unload the stretcher from the back of their truck. Uncle grabs the decapitated head of the dead man by the tuffs of hair on his head.

"I'm sorry, brother," Uncle whispers to the head before tossing it into the truck bed. It rolls around and the cigarette breaks off.

The team slowly works their way up North Zhongshan Road heading to Xiaguan District where the harbor and train station are located. They manage to pick up six corpses along the way. They lift and carry men and women. They carry dead babies with one hand. Not only are these men carrying corpses. They carry their own demons of their women being raped and their daughters and mothers being gutted by a sword.

Their scars are forever.

Chapter Fifteen

Ling sits in her hospital bed at Gulou Hospital. It has been several days since her ordeal. She is awake but has not said a word since her arrival at the hospital.

The ward is a women's ward. Only female patients are here. The only men that are allowed to stay overnight are hospital staff and western men including an Episcopalian priest named Reverend John Magee who wears his clerical collar.

He also carries a weapon of a different type. Magee carries a home movie camera that he sometimes hides from the Japanese. Documenting patient injuries with Dr. Wilson as well as filming street scenes of the city where corpse are laid bare in the open and exposed to the elements is dangerous work.

But it needs to be done. Nanjing is still cut off from the rest of the world. There is no telephone communication and no transportation system. The only communication that is available is through Japanese radio from Tokyo and a Japanese run newspaper that prints out propaganda in Chinese. Many of the westerners in Nanjing wait for the return of the western press and diplomats to the beleaguered city. They anxiously await for news from the outside world. They are desperate for letters from home.

They hope for the New Year to bring peace, gladness, and good tidings. But each day seems to bring more of the same apocalyptic gloom as more patients are brought in daily. Those who are on the mend cannot be discharged since they have no where else to go. Patients are now also refugees.

Today Wilson and Magee come into the ward with a new out patient. Dr. Wilson refers to her as a *shenzhenbing* or a half wit girl with a V-shaped gnash to the back of her neck. According to those who brought her in she foolishly fought the soldiers who were stealing her only bedding. She fought them tooth and nail. Her reward was a bayonet slice through the neck removing any muscle that supported her head.

Dr. Wilson points out the girl's injury and explains as best he could while Magee shoots footage with his camera. The doctor asks the girl to lean forward so that Magee could get a better shot of the wound. But as she moves she holds on to the doctor's shoulder. Clearly her equilibrium is off as her head just teeters on what was left of her neck.

"Do you have a name?" Magee asked the girl. She refused to speak.

"That's okay," Dr. Wilson reassured her. "You are safe here."

Ling knows who this girl is. She shuts and rubs her eyes to make sure she is seeing things right.

"Yujie?" Ling whispers to herself.

Dr. Wilson orders Chinese nurses to look after Yujie while he and Magee continue filming other patients. Next to Ling's bed is an older woman. Her face is swollen and Wilson partially exposes her legs and abdomen for Magee's camera. The woman is conscious and does not mind being filmed in this manner.

"Do you have a name?" Magee asks.

She would only give her name as Li.

"What's her story?" Magee asks Wilson.

"I'd say she's nineteen years old. She was pregnant when she arrived a few days ago." Dr. Wilson removes some of the woman's tattered and bloodied clothing so Magee could document the woman's injuries.

"Bayoneted at least thirty-seven times mainly in her abdomen and leg area. She was seven months pregnant when this happened. The baby died the day after her arrival."

Magee temporarily puts down his camera. "May God have mercy," he prayed while motioning the sign of the cross before resuming his work.

"After they stabbed her they left her to die. Her father was about to bury her when she came to. She's a fighter though. No indication of rape. I can only surmise that she fought the Japs off to get stabbed thirty-seven times."

Ling starts mumbling to herself. Magee stops filming. "And how about this young

lady?"

"Bayoneted and gang raped. Had a rip roaring case of gonorrhea a few days ago."

Magee sits on Ling's bed next to her. "May I take your picture?"

Ling consents and Magee resumes filming.

Chapter Sixteen

Ever since the fall of the city the Japanese have been itching to close all refugee camps and disband the Safety Zone. But thanks to the doggedness of Rabe, Vautrin, Wilson, and other members of the international community the Safety Zone has been allowed to remain open to all refugees. Yet the Japanese have continued to make life difficult for both westerners and Chinese who live in the Zone.

Today supposedly is December 31st. The Japanese have ordered that all refugees must register at the camps they currently reside in. Requiring refugees to register is just another way to show who is in control of the city and the people living in it.

For the past two days long lines of male refugees have lined up along Ninghai Road in front of Ginling Women's College main gate to register.

Now it is the women's turn. Long lines of women line up in front of the Central Building to register. As Minnie Vautrin writes:

> Registration took place this morning – not of the 260 college women, but of about 1,000 women between ages 17 and 30.

Yang Ayi is at the entrance sitting at a small wooden desk with pen, ink, loads of paper, and the school's official seal at hand. Before her is a long line of women waiting to register. Many of them have endured a night of hell with Japanese soldiers barging into their camp and raping them in the middle of the night. Some clearly did not get any sleep and are dazed.

A confused woman timidly approaches Yang Ayi.

"Name?"

"Zhou Feng.

"Age?"

"Twenty."

"Married?"

"Yes."

"Any children?"

"Yes. Two."

"Where are they?"

The woman does not answer. She turns her gaze to the ground.

Yang Ayi furiously writes all this information down as she continues her line of questioning oblivious to the woman's pain.

"Former place of residence?"

The woman snaps out of her daze. "Mochou District."

Yang Ayi dips her stamp on a pad of red ink before emphatically sealing this woman's paperwork with the school seal.

"Next?"

Two women converse as they wait their turn.

"Those devils took a picture of me naked!"

"Same here," says the second woman. "I hope they burn in hell."

Chapter Seventeen

January 1st, 1938. It's a new year. The snow slowly melts into the Yangtze River which has been flowing red for almost three weeks. Xuanmu and Mochou Lakes are just thawing out from their deep freeze. Blood drips from a fresh corpse and bleeds onto the melting snow, a small sign that these dark days may soon be coming to an end.

Some of the volunteers are listening to a radio broadcast from Tokyo as they pick up their equipment; shovels, stretchers, picks and keys to their vehicles. The radio broadcasts sounds of fireworks exploding and the tune Auld Lang Syne.

Rabe is able to get some of the city's services up and running but service is limited. He is able to bring electricity to parts of the city including the Zone. The Japanese have been begging him to restore power for weeks. Rabe would only do so if they promised to better control their military and provide protection for civilians. The Japanese Embassy just sent gendarmes to Ginling Women's College so Rabe acquiesces to their request.

But there is no joyous celebration in Nanjing. It is just another day at the office for the westerners and another day of gloom for the Chinese.

Today Uncle Tan's team is assigned to pick up bodies between North Zhongshan Road and Gulou, including Gulou Hospital where Uncle retires for the night to keep an eye on Ling. He parks the truck in the parking lot with some of his comrades and sleeps in the cab or in the truck bed. If it snows they pull the canvas covers over the bed.

Uncle is now a refugee. Although the restaurant has been cleared of bodies by another Red Swastika team and is structurally sound for them to keep the soup kitchen running, Uncle has been unable to return home. He has his own demons to fight. Too many memories linger in that place. The faces of his brother and father lying in a pool of

162

blood as well as his wife gutted with a broomstick are too painful.

But there are good memories as well. Aunty Shen telling him she's pregnant with their first child and just the day-to-day running of the restaurant and talking with customers makes Uncle cry and smile at the same time.

The death and destruction of the city and its citizens however, makes Uncle Tan's blood boil.

Dying is easy. It's living that's hard.

As they turn south on to Shanghai Road they find a pleasant surprise.

Commerce is slowly returning to the city. People are out setting up makeshift tables and putting out their wares for sale.

From his truck Uncle can see that survivors are selling family heirlooms such as porcelain Guanyin statues to cheaply make straw baskets. They don't have much inventory to sell but the fact that people are out and about buying and selling items is a good sign.

Uncle is looking for anyone selling food. He wants to give Ling something special for the New Year.

Only one vendor is selling food. He is out on the street with a stack of bamboo steamers piled high on a barrel containing burning coals and a pot of boiling water. Uncle stops the vehicle and gets out with his comrades to check out what this man is selling. One of the volunteers takes the lit off the top steamer.

"*Mantou* and *baozi!*" the volunteer exclaims as he smells the steamed rice cakes and buns.

"What kind of *baozi*?" asks another volunteer.

"Only *cai bao*," the skinny, wiry vendor explains. He only has buns with vegetable filling. No meat since it is still rationed.

"Any blood in it?" asks Uncle.

"No," replied the vendor. "I got clean water from the Red Cross."

"How much?"

"Brother, times are hard. Pay what you can. If you can't, then no problem. Just eat."

Under normal circumstances Uncle Tan would carry his family's money pouch to make purchases for ingredients and supplies for the restaurant. He still carries it beneath his down jacket, the only piece of clothing he owns. He unbuttons his coat and takes out the pouch. He unzips it only to find a fifty Yuan note, the last of the family's cash. He takes it out and attempts to give it to the vendor.

"One *cai bao* and one *mantou.*"

The vendor takes the food and shoves them into Uncle's hands. "No brother! Just take!"

"Take the money!"

They haggle over the transaction.

"You just told me to pay what I can," Uncle insisted forcefully. "Just take the fifty."

The embarrassed vendor reluctantly accepts the bill and thanks Uncle.

"You can use it to rebuild your home," says Uncle Tan.

"Thank you, brother."

It has been two weeks since Ling's rape. The women's ward is a buzz with activity. The women are excited and eager to do something constructive since none of them can be discharged. While some of them are still recovering and clearly are not able to move those who are able bodied are itching for something to do.

Several hospital staff members, including Nurse Hynd, John Magee, and Dr. Trimmer, arrive to make an announcement. A Chinese nurse steps up to make an announcement from a sheet of paper.

"We need people to cook and serve meals in our soup kitchens. If you are able to walk up and down stairs we need you to please stand."

A few women stand. Another nurse takes them to the soup kitchen.

"We also need people to wash clothes and linens."

More women volunteer.

"We also need women who can sew. Nurse Hynd and Dr. Trimmer have secured needles and thread and will distribute them. This is a job for those who have limited mobility. Please raise your hands if you are able."

Ling and Li, who is now called *dajie* or big sister, raise

their hands along with Yujie who now sports a crudely made neck brace cobbled together with scrap metal, bandages, and used fabric from the clothing of the dead. She slowly raises her hand.

The nurse continues reading her list. This included child care and assisting hospital staff in moving patients and, in some cases, helping staff in simple medical procedures such as cleaning and bandaging wounds.

After the announcement the hospital staff starts distributing needles and thread. Scissors is in short supply so the women have to rip cloth with their hands and break thread with their teeth. Then they are given a pile of old clothes that have already been washed and dried. Their task is to turn these clothes into bandages or rags.

"So, Sister Li. What will you do when you leave?" Ling asks as she pries a button off a jacket.

Li doesn't even flinch or look up at Ling. "Get better," she answers unequivocally.

Yujie listens to the conversation. She smiles as she continues her work.

Suddenly a nurse interrupts their work. With her is Uncle Tan who carries his gift wrapped in a cloth.

"Tan Ling. Your uncle is here."

Uncle Tan approaches the women with his gift. He sits on Ling's bed next to his niece and Yujie.

"Happy New Year girls!" Uncle greets them as he hands his bundle to Ling who unties it. She picks up the *mantou* and sniffs it. It has since gone cold but to have anything like this is a treat. No more blood. This is real food.

"*Mantou!*" Ling exclaims. "*Baozi!*"

"All for you," says Uncle.

"No, Uncle," Ling corrects him. "For everyone." She

breaks off a bite size of the bread and passes it to Yujie.

"Can you eat it?" Uncle asks her.

Yujie breaks off a morsel much smaller than Ling's. She opens her mouth and places it on her tongue before swallowing it whole. "Little," she whispers before passing the bread off to Li. The *baozi* is also passed around. Everyone on the ward, including staff, gets a piece of the tasty treats.

"Reverend Magee told us the story of Jesus feeding 5,000 people," says Ling. "I'm feeding many people too."

Uncle smiles. That is the best news he's head in as many weeks. "Girls," he says, "these foreigners are our gods. They are here to save us and the rest of China. If they ask you to do something, do it. They are good people. But I'm sure you already know."

"Yes, Uncle," the girls respond.

"And Happy New Year."

The girls swallow their tasty morsels. They will savor this for the rest of their lives.

26 D̲ ~~ZED~~
  E